TERRIBLE TIDINGS IN HILLBILLY HOLLOW

BLYTHE BAKER

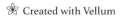 Created with Vellum

"You're taking too much on again, Emma," Grandma said in a no nonsense voice, shaking her head as she piled three extra rashers of bacon and an extra sausage onto my already full breakfast plate.

I eyed the extra food, wondering where on earth I was meant to put all of that. Sure, the country air increased my appetite in comparison to the smog of the city, but the pile I was looking at now could easily feed two people.

Maybe she was right about me taking too much on, though. I had picked up a fair bit of design work through the freelancer website recently and I felt like my business was finally starting to take off, but I still couldn't say no when Betty Blackwell had asked me to man the kettle corn stand at the Winter Carnival. The Winter Carnival was a new event for the town and it was important to everyone behind it that it was a big success. Even so, I didn't want to worry my grandmother.

"I'm not tackling too much, Grandma," I reassured her as I began to work on the mountain of food piled up before me. I smiled. "Unless you're counting this breakfast."

"You need some meat on your bones," Grandma said. "Especially if you're going to be outside in this weather. Just because Christmas is over, don't think that means it's going to be anything but freezing for the next few weeks around here. If anything, January and February are even colder in these parts." She turned to my grandpa, who was working on a breakfast even bigger than mine. "Tell her, Ed."

"Tell her what?" he asked.

"Tell her she's taking on too much," she replied with an eye roll.

"Emma, listen to your grandma," Grandpa said. He didn't sound like he really meant it. In fact, I thought he was only saying it to keep Grandma happy, so I directed my response to her rather than him.

"Honestly, Grandma. It's fine," I said. "My design work takes time, but it's not like it's stressful or anything. I enjoy doing it. It's a creative outlet for me as much as it is work. It's really just a bonus that it pays the bills. And I enjoy helping out with community stuff like the Winter Carnival. And don't forget that while I'm manning the kettle corn stand, I won't be doing anything else for the Historical Society because I'm helping with fundraising on their behalf. So it's not like I've taken on anything extra. I've just refocused my time."

Grandma didn't look convinced, but she let it go. Almost.

"Just know that you're allowed to say no to things, Emma," she replied.

Except this ridiculously big breakfast, I thought to myself with a smile. Grandma had always been a feeder, a habit which I had hoped she had outgrown since I left town, but if anything, it had only gotten worse now that I was back in Hillbilly Hollow for good.

"I know I can refuse, Grandma. And if it gets to be too

much for me, I will say no to extra projects. I promise," I told her.

Snowball, my little white goat that acted more like a loyal dog than a goat, saved me from further questioning. She popped out from underneath the table with half a sausage in her mouth and made us all laugh.

"Where did you get that, Snowball?" I asked through my laughter.

"I gave it to her," Grandma admitted. "I figured if I fed her a sausage, she might leave my linens alone. You know yesterday I had to chase her through the house to get my table cloth back? She whipped it right off the table and ran."

We all laughed some more.

Snowball finished her sausage and came over to stand beside me. She bleated loudly and rubbed her head on my knee. I reached down and scratched the top of her head.

Then I ate another couple forkfuls of breakfast, before having to admit defeat long before the meal was even half gone. I put my fork down and sat back with a sigh.

"I'm sorry, Grandma. I can't eat another thing," I said, rubbing my tummy.

"Put the leftovers in Betsy's bucket," Grandpa said. "She won't turn them down."

Betsy was my grandpa's prize winning pig and she got all of the house leftovers. Knowing Grandma had a massive soft spot for Betsy, I smiled at Grandpa. Now that he had suggested Betsy should have the extra scraps, Grandma wouldn't insist I eat more. Grandpa caught my eye and gave me a wink.

All the same, I stood up quickly and grabbed my plate before Grandma could make even a small protest. I headed for the backyard, hearing Snowball scramble to her feet and follow me out through the door. I breathed in the cold air, feeling my cheeks tingle at the biting chill. I would definitely need to wrap up warm today. It would be my first day volunteering at the Winter Carnival and I didn't want to spend it sitting freezing cold at my stall.

"I reckon it's about time I invested in some thermal underwear," I said to Snowball as I scraped my plate into Betsy's bucket.

Snowball bleated back at me and I grinned to myself.

"You're right, Snowball. I'm not ninety and I would die at the thought of Billy finding out I wear thermal underwear."

She bleated again, almost as though she was relieved I had seen sense, as I hurried back to the house. I was already wearing a t-shirt with a thick angora sweater over it and a pair of denim jeans. I figured with my nice warm coat, gloves, a scarf and a hat, I'd be fine at the carnival today. I also remembered Betty Blackwell telling me that it could get kind of hot at the kettle corn stand. If I did get too hot, at least I had easy layers to remove. I suspected Betty had said that just to convince me to work the stand, though.

I washed my plate at the sink and then turned to my grandparents.

"Well, I'd better be going. I don't want to get in Betty's bad books on my first day," I said.

"Good thinking. Betty still talks about how you were constantly late for the Christmas Garden event," Grandpa answered.

I rolled my eyes good naturedly. That was Betty all over. Of course, I had seen a different side to her, a softer side, when she had caught a grieving young mother named Beth vandalising the Christmas Garden last month. Rather than handing the woman over to the police, Betty had instead understood her motives and welcomed her into our efforts as a new volunteer for the Historical Society. But all of that aside, Betty was still an old battleaxe, and it was never a good idea to get too many pages deep into her bad books.

I said my goodbyes, including a last chin scratch for Snowball, and then I went out into the hallway and put on my coat, hat, scarf and gloves. I grabbed the keys for the old farm truck and hurried to it. At least last month's snow had mostly gone now. There was still the odd patch on some of the lesser-used roads, but for the most part, the ground was clear again. It was just icy cold. I was grateful it wasn't raining either. People would turn out for the carnival in the cold, I was sure, but rain would put so many of them off, especially those with young children.

I drove through the town. The carnival was being held on the outskirts of the town on land belonging to Hugh Masterton, a long time supporter of the charity and community initiatives ran in Hillbilly Hollow, who had instantly volunteered his land for free when the subject of a Winter Carnival came up.

As I reached the end of the last block of houses, I got my first glimpse of the Ferris wheel in the distance, towering over the rest of the carnival. When I reached the parking area, I wound my window down an inch and was instantly rewarded with the smell of frying onions and burgers, fresh cotton candy and donuts, all mingling together to bring the carnival to life. I could hear the *thump thump thump* of music playing on some of the rides.

The town council had really gone to town on this carnival. They had rented a Ferris wheel, bumper cars, waltzers and even a small roller coaster, plus the ride operators. There was a helter skelter and a few smaller rides for the little ones too. The various concession stands and game booths had all been allocated to charities and local businesses to promote their wares and raise money.

I felt a tingle of excitement run through me as I parked, rolled the window back up and got out of the truck. The music here was louder and the way all the cheerful noises rolled together was definitely enough to attract visitors. Once evening came and all the rides and stands were lit up, it would be even more attractive, I knew. The carnival wouldn't be open to the public for another forty-five minutes, but already there were families milling around, waiting for the gates to open. Blasting out the music early to get people's attention and remind them this was the carnival's opening day had been a good idea, it seemed.

I hurried around to the side gate where Betty had told me to enter when I was on duty. The gate was guarded by one of Sheriff Tucker's deputies, who would probably be patrolling the carnival over the next few hours. I felt police presence was unnecessary, but after the recent murder at the Christmas Garden, it made sense that security for this new event would be a priority. Not that any of Tucker's deputies would be much use in an emergency. Like the handsome sheriff himself, most of them were well-intentioned but not the brightest or the most experienced at dealing with serious crime. Still, if nothing else, they would deter teenage drinking or fights, I figured, and surely those were the worst things that could happen at a carnival.

The deputy recognised me and opened the gate, pointing me in the direction of the "administration building," as he called it. In fact, it was the same moveable marquee we had used for the Christmas Garden.

I walked in to see Betty Blackwell, the Historical Society's president, and her second in command, Patty Harris, sitting behind a desk, checking volunteers' names off their lists. People bustled in and out of the marquee, double-checking where they needed to be and asking questions that both Betty and Patty reeled off the answers to like pros.

The two women were similar in appearance, both being tall and slim older ladies with greying hair. But while Patty wore her curls in a relaxed, short style, Betty's hair was scraped back in a tight bun that matched her high-collared shirt and spotless slacks. There was, as usual, a pencil tucked behind Betty's ear, something I suspected she kept there all the time, just because it made her look busy and official.

I reached the front of the little line, and Betty smiled as I approached her.

"On time for once," she commented approvingly.

I resisted the urge to point out that I was nearly always punctual. Instead, I just smiled and nodded. I was learning to choose my battles with Betty, and this one I could let go.

Betty pointed behind herself, toward a small white screen.

"Your uniform is behind there," she said. "Off you go to change."

Uniform? Change?

"Why do I need a uniform?" I asked. "Most other people aren't wearing one."

"Most other people here aren't representing the Historical Society. We want to show everyone exactly who we are," she replied.

I sighed but it could be worse. I'd seen lots of fund raisers for the Historical Society around town before, and the volunteers typically wore black pants and a yellow polo shirt in summer, or a yellow sweatshirt in winter. It was another point that wasn't worth arguing, so I made my way around Betty's desk and over to the screen. I ducked behind it and my jaw dropped when I saw my so-called uniform.

"I'm not wearing that," I shouted out to Betty, my eyes not leaving the outfit.

There were no pants or sweatshirts in sight. Instead, there was an ankle-length pink dress with puffy sleeves and a white pinafore over the top. The most offensive part of the outfit was the matching pink bonnet.

I was used to dressing as a nineteenth century nurse during old fort days, but that was at old Fort Harris, where all the volunteers were in prairie costumes. Dressing crazy out in the real world was a whole other thing.

The screen rustled as Betty made her way back.

"Why ever wouldn't you wear it?" she asked. "It's a lovely dress and historically what a woman would have worn in the olden days."

"But this isn't the nineteenth century," I protested.

"And Santa isn't real, but you had no problem with pretending during the Christmas Garden. Think of this the same as that. You're bringing a little magic to an otherwise dull event."

How could she think a carnival was dull? Only Betty would fail to see that the rides, the sounds, the smells, and the lights were the magic of a carnival, not what anybody was wearing.

"I'm not wearing it," I said again.

"Beth will be upset to hear that," Betty said.

"Beth? What's this got to do with Beth?" I asked.

"Since she's the Historical Society's newest volunteer, I've taken her under my wing, as you know," Betty explained.

I rubbed my hand over my lips to cover my smile. I knew alright. Beth had spent many a phone call telling me about how she was going to scream if Betty told her one more time that she was doing everything wrong. She went along with it, though, grateful to Betty for a second chance and a way to be involved with the community again. A lot of people might have turned Beth in, after catching her vandalizing the displays during the Christmas Garden event, but Betty had been uncharacteristically kind when she learned the reasons behind Beth's actions.

"This costume was Beth's idea. And she spent hours making it," Betty went on.

"She sewed this?" I asked, impressed despite myself.

Betty nodded. "Yes. But if it's not good enough for you, I'm sure she'll understand."

Betty said this in a tone that indicated Beth definitely wouldn't understand.

I heard myself sigh. "Fine. I'll wear it."

Betty beamed. "That's my girl," she said. She glanced at her watch. "Quickly now. It's nearly time you were at your post."

She flounced back away, leaving me glaring at her receding back.

I sighed again and shook my head as I began to strip off my coat and all my other layers. I finally managed to get into the dress and bonnet. The darned bonnet. Beth and I were going to have some serious words about this, I decided.

I edged out from behind the screen, trying to make myself as small and inconspicuous as possible. Not an easy feat the way I was dressed.

Betty clapped her hands together in delight when she saw me. "Oh, Emma, you look adorable," she cooed.

Every eye in the marquee was suddenly on me and I felt my cheeks heat up as I blushed crimson.

Betty either didn't notice my discomfort or, more likely, didn't care about it.

"Doesn't she look adorable, Patty?" Betty asked at a volume that attracted even more attention.

Patty nodded and beamed at me. "Perfection," she announced.

"Where abouts is the stand?" I asked through gritted teeth, just wanting to get away from the eyes that were on me.

Betty gave me directions to the kettle corn stand and went once more over the procedure for making the kettle corn, something she had explained to me five times already, even though I had made it clear to her earlier that I knew how to do it already. It was something Grandma had taught me when I was a little girl and it wasn't complicated enough to forget.

I hurried through the carnival, no longer paying attention to the magic all around me, just wanting to get to my stand, where I could duck behind the counter and have the majority of me hidden. As I moved, I felt the chill wind go straight up my skirt. It seemed I was going to have to give in and get some thermal underwear, after all.

I reached my stand, only to discover that the word "stand" was far from accurate. It was actually a small, open tent. There was an enormous cast iron cauldron for mixing the kettle corn. Hidden behind it were bags and bags of popcorn and almost as many bags of sugar. There was also a large wooden spoon for stirring and stacks of cardboard pouches for serving the treat in. The trick was to always be stirring the popcorn and sugar together to keep the mixture sticky and sweet.

Beside the cauldron was a fold-out wooden chair. I shuddered when I realized I would be perched there, my embarrassing costume in open view of everyone who walked past. And because the stall was placed between the waltzers and the Ferris wheel, I would be in a prime spot for a constant flow of people.

I had to hand it to Betty; it was a good location. She had no doubt pulled strings and bullied someone else into giving the Historical Society such a prestigious spot. If I had been wearing my own clothes, I would have admired her. As it was, I detested having to sit somewhere so public while I looked so utterly stupid.

Still, there was no way out of it. I got everything set up. Then I sat down in the chair and began to stir the kettle corn. It was kind of therapeutic in a way, just a constant, easy motion. The carnival opened on time and, within an hour, the place was swinging. The rides were going constantly and there were lines at most of the stalls and game booths. The next two hours flew by in a blur of serving excited children and their parents. Everyone was rushing around, wanting to get to the next attraction, and apart from the odd comment, people mostly kept quiet about my costume, which suited me just fine. I only wished I wasn't so cold from the wind billowing up my skirt.

Once things quietened down a little bit, I dug my cell phone out of the pinafore pocket and sent a quick text to my best friend Suzy.

ME: Hey. Let's meet up and go baby shopping after I finish at the carnival today.

NOW SEVERAL MONTHS PREGNANT, Suzy had been asking me for days to go shopping with her for furniture for the baby's nursery. I was going to be in that part of town today anyway to get some thermal underwear to last me for the rest of the carnival. So I figured this would be a good day for the baby shopping too. It would be nice to catch up with Suzy, who I'd barely seen since Christmas, as we were both busy with work and family things lately.

Suzy's reply came back to me in seconds.

SUZY: U R on. What time? Oh and by the way, nice dress and even nicer hat.

ME: Let's meet at 5:30. And who told U about my bonnet?

SUZY: 1 of the regular customers at my shop saw U earlier. Don't worry. She said U look adorable. See U in a bit.

I PUSHED my cell phone back into my pocket, silently cursing Beth and her silly costume. She would be taking shifts manning the stall too, so why she had suggested such a ridiculous outfit was beyond me.

I decided to try and put the costume out of my mind. I found that, other than the constant breeze up my skirt, it was really quite easy to get caught up in the excitement of the carnival once more. The rest of my shift at the booth flew by.

2

A fellow volunteer named Danny Clarke came to relieve me from my post when my shift in the kettle corn stall was over.

I was dismayed to see his costume, if it could be called a costume at all. He wore an ordinary black suit and white button-down shirt, the only nod to a truly historical feel being the top hat perched precariously on his head. He looked vaguely like a shorter, stockier Abraham Lincoln, minus the beard. He also looked much warmer and more comfortable than me.

He gave me a look of sympathy when he saw my outfit.

"Lovely, isn't it?" I asked sarcastically, giving him a twirl.

"You know what Betty's like," he replied. "It's easier just to go along with it, right?"

I nodded. I didn't want to get into the whole thing about it being Beth's idea. I just wanted to return to the marquee and get back into my own clothes. It would be nice to spend some time with no draft up my skirt and to lose the floppy-brimmed bonnet.

"How did you get away with wearing a modern suit? The top hat isn't so bad." I laughed.

"I have no idea. I'm just grateful," Danny said, laughing back.

"I take it Betty has already given you a lecture about how the cauldron works, the ratio of the mixture, and the constant stirring?" I asked.

Danny nodded and smiled.

"Yes, but only four times, so who knows whether I can actually remember it or not?"

I quickly showed him where everything was kept and then I hurried off to the marquee, trying to keep my head down and not meet anyone's eyes. Just because everyone already seemed to know I was wearing the hideous dress, didn't mean they had to get a front row view of it.

It was quiet when I finally got back to the marquee. Patty was still behind the desk, but there was no sign of Betty. I nodded a greeting to Patty and rushed behind the screen before quickly shedding my outfit and getting into my own clothes again. I breathed a sigh of relief at their familiar feel against my skin.

I wondered if I could hide the prairie costume and feign innocence at its disappearance. But then I remembered Beth had made it, and doing something like that might make her feel like an outsider once more. *Darn it, Beth, why did you have to come up with this whole costume idea?*

I checked my wristwatch, the historical inaccuracy of which Betty had overlooked, allowing me to keep it on. I had half an hour to kill before I had to go and meet Suzy.

I knew instantly what I would do with the time. I wanted to ride on the Ferris wheel. I'd been tempted to abandon my post to enjoy the ride ever since it had opened earlier. I might have done it too, if I'd been dressed in my normal clothes before. The Ferris wheel always brought back fond memories from my childhood, memories of walking through carnivals and fairs similar to this one, feeling the magic in the air. I used to cling to Grandma's hand, my eyes wide with excitement. My first stop was always the Ferris wheel.

I no longer held Grandma's hand, but the rest hadn't changed. As I ducked through the crowd, I could feel the magic in the air, and I was sure my eyes glistened with joy just like they had as a kid.

I reached the Ferris wheel and stood in line, looking up at the tall structure as it spun around. The flashing lights looked really good now that darkness was beginning to fall. Another hour or so and the whole carnival would be lit up beautifully.

I could hear squeals of excitement as the Ferris wheel swept the riders up into the air and then brought them back down again. One teenage girl screamed in alarm high above me, as her date rocked their carriage. I couldn't help smiling, pulled back into a memory of something similar happening to me at that age. The world moved on but some things never changed.

I remembered one summer day when Suzy, Billy and I had gone on a day trip into town and had stumbled across a carnival. We'd ridden the ghost train and gotten well and truly spooked, then we'd ridden the Ferris wheel. As we neared the top, Billy had rocked the carriage until Suzy and I screamed at him to stop, sure we would plunge to our deaths. Billy had laughed, telling us we were strapped in and couldn't fall out. He'd gotten a playful glint in his eye and said the car we were riding in could come loose, though. That had gotten us both screaming again.

The Ferris wheel before me started to slow down. When

it came to a stop, I was pulled out of my happy memories and back into the present. The rocking carriage was now halfway down and the girl's screams were getting louder as the carriage tipped wildly. The first carriage was opened and the riders hopped down, allowing the next people to get on board. This continued on. Before long, I was next in line.

"Just one, love?" the man operating the ride asked me.

I nodded.

"Two dollars please," he said.

I paid him and waited for him to open up the carriage. The teenage couple got out of the car, the girl looking more happy than shaken. She was laughing as they made their way off the platform, but telling her date off for tormenting her.

I got into the car, and the operator snapped the safety bar closed. With a lurch, I was moved up one place and was brought to an abrupt stop as the next riders were loaded in. When I neared the top, I leaned over the side of the car to look down on the carnival. I'd never feared heights, and I enjoyed the view.

I was high enough that I couldn't make out individual faces in the crowd below. I had no idea who the people on the ground were but I could pick out the occasional excited squeal of a child and the laughter of families as they walked around. I spotted a bright red coat that stood out from the rest, and a bright yellow bobble hat. I looked around and saw the bumper cars banging into each other, the waltzers spinning away and the constant flow of the crowd. I glanced out towards the parking lot to see how busy it was there and whether more people were arriving.

My attention was caught by two men in the parking lot. Their arms were gesticulating wildly and they appeared to be in a heated argument, as they shoved at each other.

Although I couldn't see their faces or hear what they were saying, their posturing was enough to tell me the fight wasn't going to end well.

I squinted, trying to make out the faces of the men, but it was no use. One of them wore a bright orange sweater that would be hard to miss in a crowd. I told myself I could easily find out who he was when I got back on the ground and then ask Grandma later if he was rumored to have bad blood with anyone. Small town life was getting to me, and local gossip was becoming something I looked forward to.

The car began to move up another notch and it lurched forward alarmingly, so that I sat back quickly, my heart pounding at the sensation of almost falling. I laughed nervously. It had served me right for leaning forward against the rail just to be nosey.

That didn't stop me leaning over for another look, though. The two men were still among the parked cars and still shouting at each other, but it seemed that was all that would happen. If the fight was going to get more physical than shoving, it would have happened by now.

My cell phone buzzed and I did a quick mental calculation to work out whether I had time to reply to the incoming text message before the ride started properly. Figuring I had a couple minutes yet, I pulled the phone out of my pocket and smiled when I saw Billy's name on the screen.

I still couldn't believe I had resisted dating Billy for so long. He was a single, attractive doctor with a reliable job running the local clinic. He was also sweet, charming, and funny, and had been one of my best friends since childhood. I had been so afraid of losing him as a friend that I had ignored our mutual attraction for a long time. Luckily, he had been persistent until, eventually, I'd given in. We had been dating for a few weeks now and I was happy with the relationship. I knew in my heart it wouldn't go wrong. We were made for each other and always had been. It had just taken me far too long to see it.

I opened the text message.

BILLY: Hey there, Gorgeous. Fancy dinner with a handsome doctor?

I WAS DISAPPOINTED that I would have to turn him down, but I already had plans with Suzy. I didn't see anywhere near enough of her as it was. I couldn't cancel on her so close to the time we were due to meet, especially not when I hadn't seen her in what felt like forever.

ME: Sorry, Doctor Billy. I already have a date for tonight.

I REALIZED I had moved right over the top of the Ferris wheel and was almost back down to the ground, so I pushed my cell phone back into my pocket and waited for the ride to start. I pictured Billy's face as he read my text. He would grin and shake his head, I knew, understanding that I was only teasing about having a different date. A part of me hoped he would be a little disappointed that I couldn't make it tonight, just like I was a little disappointed too.

All thoughts of Billy left me as the ride started up properly. I was plunged towards the ground before being swept back up into the air. My stomach rolled delightfully and I laughed, enjoying the sensation of weightlessness.

The ride was over far too quickly and I debated going

again. But the line was long and I had to get going anyway. I wanted to pop in at a used bookstore on my way to meet Suzy and I was already cutting it fine.

I hopped off the ride, and thanked the operator. It was only as I was heading for my truck that I remembered my conversation with Billy. I got my cell phone back out to see a waiting text message from him.

BILLY: Shame. I had big plans 4 us …

ME: And I have big plans with Suzy. Let's do your thing tomorrow evening?

BILLY: Deal.

HE SENT me an emoji heart and I smiled to myself.

As I reached the parking lot, I remembered the argument I had seen earlier. I scanned the place, looking for the men who had been quarrelling. I would have seen the orange sweater at one hundred paces, but there was no sign of it now. The only people in the parking lot besides myself was a family with three excited looking children, all bundled up in winter coats and ready for the carnival. The only parts of them visible were their red, happy faces. I smiled at them and the smallest child waved at me. I waved back as I reached my truck.

When I got in, I started the engine and ran the heater, tucking my hands into my arm pits until the truck finally began to warm up. I checked my watch. I still had enough time to get to the book store before meeting Suzy.

As I drove away from the carnival, I thought that the first day had been a huge success. The event would only get better as word spread and people visited from the neighbouring towns too. I was already in love with the atmosphere of the place, and it felt good to be involved in another fund raising effort for the Historical Society.

Who knew? Maybe I'd even come to love my pink prairie costume.

3

I parked the truck at a convenient spot at the end of Main Street. The vehicle was usually next to impossible to park there, but a similar sized truck was just pulling out as I arrived and I ducked into that spot.

I hopped out of the truck and instantly felt the cold air biting my face as I left the warmth of the cab behind. I tucked my chin further down into my scarf, pulling it up over my nose and mouth. The heat of my breath helped to warm my chin and lips as I began to hurry along Main Street. My fast pace soon had me warm enough that I wasn't shivering anymore.

I ducked into a side street, the one I was sure Grandma had meant when she gave me directions to the used bookstore. Although I had been back in town for some time, I'd never had reason to go to the bookstore before. I hurried along the side street, scanning the signs above the shop doorways as I went.

There it was. Caldwell's Used Books.

I opened the door, smiling to myself at the dinging

sound of the old fashioned bell that alerted the store owners to someone coming in. I pulled the door shut behind me, keeping the wind out, and felt the warmth of the inside of the shop immediately.

I looked around. A sour-faced man stood behind the counter looking down the spines of a huge stack of books that perched precariously on the end of the counter next to an old-fashioned cash register. He glared at me and I looked quickly away. He didn't seem like the sort who was particularly focused on customer service, so rather than asking if he carried the book I wanted, I instead looked at the hanging signs on the ceiling and made my way to the children's section.

I wanted to surprise Suzy by getting her baby a copy of The Sleepy Puppy, a picture book we had both loved as young girls. I was pretty sure it was out of print and could only be purchased used. But as I scanned the shelves, I didn't see what I was looking for. There were hundreds of children's books in the store, and I was worried that I would either miss the puppy book, or spend so long looking for it that Suzy would be annoyed about how late I was and my surprise would be ruined.

I knew I would have to brave talking to the man with the sour face. I headed for the front counter, telling myself permanent annoyance might just be his natural expression. Some people looked angry when they were perfectly happy. It was just the way they were. After all, surely he had to be reasonably friendly to work somewhere like this. I should give him the benefit of the doubt.

I peered through the shelves as I approached the counter. The man looked vaguely familiar to me, with his skinny frame, stooped shoulders, and salt and pepper hair, but I couldn't place where I knew him from. I was certain I would remember someone so grumpy.

He had stopped reading the spines now and was moving books from the large stack on the counter to a nearby shelf. He muttered to himself as he went, and I noticed he walked with a limp. Maybe that was why he looked so miserable. Maybe he was in a lot of pain. As I watched him, though, I realized his limp was moving from leg to leg as he went. Sometimes he limped on the right side, other times on the left. It was strange to watch and I couldn't help but wonder why he was walking that way. It was as though the limp was fake. Surely it had to be. No pain moved from side to side so quickly like that.

The man turned around, still looking every bit as annoyed as he had when I first came into the store, perhaps now because he could feel my eyes on him. I realized I had been caught staring. I felt my face flush with embarrassment, and I was stuttering as I stepped from behind the shelf.

"Oh. Um. Hi. I-I'm sorry to disturb you. I was just waiting until you were finished," I said.

"I'm never finished. There's always something else to do," he replied gruffly, doing nothing to put me at ease or make me feel like my question was going to be a welcome one.

"I was wondering if you had a copy of The Sleepy Puppy?" I asked. "I wanted it for—"

He shrugged and turned away before I could finish my sentence. He clearly wasn't interested in my question, let alone my reason for wanting the book.

"If we do, it'll be back there in the children's section," he replied, waving his arm in the general direction I had just come from. He must have known I'd already been down there and looked.

It was clear I was being dismissed as a nuisance. Normally, I would take the hint, and while I would fume inside, I would smile meekly and go to find the darned thing myself. There was something about this man that got under my skin, though. Something about his brusque manner and casual dismissal made me angry, and I decided I wasn't going to let him brush me aside quite that easily.

I forced my tone to remain light and breezy when I replied, "Thank you, but I'm in kind of a hurry, so if you would be so helpful as to grab me a copy, that would be great."

He turned to face me, making no effort to hide his sullen expression. Then he gave an exaggerated sigh and moved as slowly as possible towards a curtain behind the counter. I knew it wasn't because of the limp – that was still switching from one leg to the other, so it obviously wasn't bothering him much.

"Mildred? Get out here. Some woman who thinks her time is more important than ours can't seem to find what she's looking for."

He didn't glance back to see me staring in open-mouthed shock at his attitude. Instead, he swept through the curtain and was gone, leaving me alone in the store. I almost left, assuming this Mildred person would be as bad as he was. But as I reached the door, the curtain swished and she appeared.

"Oh, please don't leave," she said, hurrying to my side. She glanced back, making sure we were alone. "I apologise for Clayton. Don't take it personally. He's like that with everyone. You would think he hated this place, but it's his store, so I can only assume he hates people." She leaned closer, whispering in a conspiratorial tone. "I have a theory that his mother didn't hug him enough as a child."

I grinned, liking this woman right away. She seemed to be the polar opposite to Clayton. She looked like she was about the same age as my Grandma, and her eyes sparkled with intelligence as she smiled. She was wearing a sensible blouse and skirt over tights so thick they were almost pants. Over the blouse she wore a pink cardigan buttoned almost all the way up to her neck. A pair of thick-lensed glasses hung from a cord around her neck.

"How does he ever keep any customers?" I asked.

Mildred beamed. "Because he has me as his long-suffering assistant. Now, what were you looking for?"

"The Sleepy Puppy," I told her.

She lead me towards the children's section. Then she looked back, checking once more that we were still alone.

"If you think Clayton's rude to customers, you don't want to try working for him," she whispered.

"So why do you stay?" I asked, wondering why she would put up with Clayton and his grouchy attitude.

"It's partly because of my love for books. I used to be a librarian, you know. I'm too old for that now. Too much of this new fangled technology involved. But I still love being around old books. It's the smell and the memories. But I have to keep Clayton Caldwell happy, because I don't just work here. I live in the apartment above the store too, and he's made it perfectly clear that the work and the lodging go hand in hand."

"I see," I said. "What a horrible position to be in."

"Well, I don't think I'll have to put up with it much longer," she said, looking sad. "Rumor has it Clayton's about to inherit a lot of money from a dead relative. If that happens, I'm afraid he'll sell the whole property altogether. I don't know what will become of me then. But it's only gossip. Maybe it will never happen."

Mildred had arrived at the section she needed and now she reached out and put her hand straight on the book. It was clear she knew the store and its stock a lot better than Clayton did.

She handed the hardback to me and asked, "Is this the one?"

I smiled and nodded, relieved. "Yes, thank you! It's a surprise for my best friend. She's expecting, and this book was one we both loved as kids."

Leading me back towards the counter, she said over her shoulder, "A book is so much more than the words inside, isn't it? It's often the memories attached that make it so special."

I nodded agreement, as she rang my price into the register and I fished around inside my purse for the money. I paid her.

While she was wrapping the book I said, "Thanks again for your help. And I really hope the rumor you're worried about is just that."

She glanced at the curtain, checking that the coast was clear. "Clayton is sure he's going to get lots of money anyway, with or without that inheritance. He's in the middle of suing someone now for an injury, although it's completely fake, if you ask me. I reckon he went into a store and just pretended to fall down. But the business owner he's blaming is no idiot and he refuses to pay without going through the courts. I don't think Clayton will win that case. He can't remember for two seconds which side his limp is meant to be on."

"Yeah, I noticed," I confided.

"It's not the first time he's done this, bringing some sort of lawsuit against a local businessman just to extort money.

He's never won yet and I doubt this one will be any different."

"Mildred!" Clayton's voice suddenly shouted through the curtain. "It's time to stop gossiping and get back to work! Those books aren't going to catalogue themselves!"

I recoiled from the harsh tone, but Mildred just rolled her eyes and turned her head towards the curtain.

"Coming," she called in a voice that contained none of the anger I was sure she must feel.

She smiled at me and handed me the wrapped book. "Enjoy the rest of your day," she said.

"You too," I answered.

If that's even possible, I mentally added, as she hurried through the curtain and back into the evil realm of Clayton Caldwell.

I pushed the shop door open and stepped out into the street, then headed back toward my meeting point with Suzy. I had debated leaving the bookstore door open and letting the icy cold air into the shop. But that was petty, plus it would make Mildred cold too.

I couldn't help but think how awful it must be for poor Mildred, being at the mercy of such an unpleasant man all of the time. And to think he might sell up and evict her if his inheritance came through! Even if the inheritance proved to be an empty rumor and he didn't win his court case either, it was still horrible if he had even hinted to the old woman that he would sell her home out from under her.

As I reached Main Street, I thought of Clayton Caldwell's grouchy appearance once more and got that feeling again. The feeling that there was something familiar about him. I wondered if Grandma had pointed him out to me around town at some time, but I couldn't recall such an incident. I was sure if she had pointed him out, Grandma would also have told me about the rumors surrounding him. She certainly would have known them. She loved a good gossip, my grandma.

Just when I was about to decide I must be mistaken about having seen Clayton before, it suddenly came to me where I recognised the man from. It wasn't his face I had recognised – it was his distinctive bright orange sweater. I had seen it in the parking lot at the carnival. He was one of the two men I had witnessed arguing while I was up on the Ferris wheel.

He must have taken a shortcut through the carnival parking lot on his way to work this evening and that was how he'd gotten to the bookshop before me. By the time my ride had finished and I had gotten off, then made my way to the parking lot and waited for the truck to heat up before driving to the shop, he could easily have walked the short distance to the store.

Yes, that made sense. The explanation satisfied my curiosity about why I recognised Clayton, but it also made me wonder about the argument. Who was the other angry man Clayton had encountered and what was their fight about? I tried to summon up a mental picture of the other man, but my memory of him was fuzzy. Nothing about him had stood out to me at the time. If Clayton hadn't been wearing such a bright sweater I probably wouldn't have remembered him either.

I figured the other man in the argument could be pretty much anyone who'd had the displeasure of dealing with Clayton Caldwell. If my brief encounter with him and Mildred's talk about him was anything to go by, it would be hard to find someone who wouldn't have a bone to pick with the greedy, bad-tempered bookshop owner.

I decided to put all these nosey questions out of my

mind. I had done enough digging for gossip for one day. If there was anything worth knowing about the fight in the parking lot, Grandma would surely hear of it and pass on the details.

Meanwhile, I just wanted to concentrate on having a good visit with Suzy.

4

I hurried along Main Street, trying to resist looking at the displays in the shop windows as I passed, worried I would spot something interesting and lose track of the time. I vaguely was aware of spotting some thermal underwear in one of the stores my grandma frequented which I'd promised myself never to venture into. I knew I had to break that promise very soon though. The memory of the breeze sweeping up my costume at the carnival was too fresh to ignore. I would rather swallow my pride than freeze to death at the stall tomorrow.

I knew I could sneak in there and buy them now, so Suzy never even had to know my shameful underwear secret. But if I did that I'd be late to meet her. Then I'd end up explaining the reason to her anyway, so she'd know where I'd been and why I was late. I was going to have to accept that this was something Suzy and I would share. She knew when to keep her mouth shut, at least, and this was definitely one of those times. It was one thing having the whole town laughing at my prairie costume. I drew the line at the idea of them all laughing at my underwear.

When I arrived at the baby boutique ahead of Suzy, I couldn't help but smile. My friend must have been delayed with closing up her own clothing shop, Posh Closet, for the night. I'd been so paranoid I'd be late, and yet Suzy was known for never being on time for anything.

I stood on the sidewalk in front of the store, peering inside through the display window. I smiled to myself when I saw the tiny white baby jumpers, cribs surrounded by pale taffeta, and various stuffed animals. It was all so small and cute. I felt myself getting broody and shook my head.

Easy there, Emma. You've been dating Billy for five minutes. Let's not go getting ahead of yourself.

I took a step back to look up at the store's signage. It was a store I'd never really taken much notice of before now. I gasped when I saw the sign.

The Baby Boutique by Charlotte Caldwell.

Caldwell as in Clayton Caldwell? Well, that was just great. I hoped Charlotte was a bit nicer than Clayton. Was she his sister?

I saw Suzy hurrying up Main Street, so I put the Caldwells out of my mind.

"Hi," I said as she arrived at my side, flustered and rushing as always.

She pulled me into a hug. "Hey, how are you? Sorry I'm late. I got caught up at the shop."

"It's fine. I would be more worried if you were on time than I am when you're late," I said, laughing.

"Ah, my reputation precedes me as always." She grinned.

"I've got something for you," I told her, handing her the wrapped book.

She took it and smiled quizzically at me.

"Go on. Open it," I urged.

She didn't need telling twice. She ripped the paper off the book and her face lit up when she saw it.

"It's more of a gift for the baby really," I said. "Do you like it?"

"Like it? I love it! Oh, Emma, it's perfect," she said, pulling me into another tight embrace. "Little Aaron or Harley is going to adore it as much as we did when we were little. Do you remember? Whenever we were at each other's houses, we'd beg my mom or your grandma to read it to us. They must have known the story by heart, after awhile."

"I know. I can still see the face they pulled. The one that was meant to be a smile but was more an accepting grimace," I said.

Then I changed the subject. "So, Aaron or Harley? You have names now?"

Suzy waved her hand and laughed.

"Yes, but whether or not they'll stay the same is anyone's guess. We're onto name four for girls and name three for boys. We've had Jackson and George if it's a boy and Rachel, Scarlet, and Ava for a girl. Now it's Aaron or Harley. Do you like them?"

I nodded. "I love them."

"Good. Now let's get inside. I'm freezing here."

She went to step inside the store and I put my hand on her arm, stopping her for a moment. I pointed up to the sign.

"Charlotte Caldwell. Is she related to Clayton Caldwell, the bookstore owner?" I asked.

Suzy nodded. "Yeah. I think they're some relation to each other, but I don't really know for sure. I've always just assumed because of the name, to be honest. Why are you suddenly interested in Clayton Caldwell?" Her face broke into a suggestive smile and she waggled her eyebrows.

"Bored of Billy? Looking for an alternative for the odd date here and there?"

"Eww! No," I said and laughed. "I was just in his bookstore getting your book. He's quite a character, isn't he?"

"A character is one way of putting it. Not quite as strong as the words I'd use. Don't worry, though, Charlotte isn't quite as bad as him. Although... I do sometimes wonder why she chose to run a baby boutique when it's clear she's not a fan of babies or children. But her stuff is the nicest in town, so what can you do? Now are we going to stand out here comparing the whole town's family trees, or are we going to go in there and do some serious shopping?"

"Serious shopping it is." I laughed.

Suzy's enthusiasm was infectious as she pulled me into the store. I told myself that's all it was, as I looked at the tiny things in the boutique and felt my insides turn to mush.

I almost believed myself, too. Almost.

5

We walked into the store and Suzy immediately squealed with excitement, clapped her hands together and pulled me over to a sweet little bassinet. It hung from a white stand and above and around it hung pale taffeta adorned with tiny silver stars. Suzy beamed at the item like a young child seeing her first Christmas tree.

"What do you think?" she asked me, gently caressing the taffeta between her fingers.

Her face shone with excitement and I already knew she would be buying the bassinet, regardless of my thoughts on the matter. I knew deep down I wasn't here to give my real opinion. I was here so Suzy had someone to share her excitement with. I was okay with that. It was her first baby and she should be excited. I had to admit I was excited myself to be a part of it all.

"I love it." I grinned.

She looked at the price tag, winced a little, and then shrugged.

"Oh well. What's a few hundred hours of overtime and an overdraft in the face of everything being beautiful for little Aaron or Harley?" she asked. "It has to be done right. I mean, the little one is our first baby and everything has to be perfect, doesn't it?"

I didn't get a chance to answer before she gasped and moved off towards a white dresser with little yellow handles crafted into the shapes of ducks.

The door to the store opened and I turned away from Suzy for a moment to see who had entered. A young couple had come in. The lady carried a baby in a sling and a girl of around three years old clung happily to her dad's hand, looking up at him and chattering away.

Charlotte appeared from behind a curtain as soon as the family descended on the store. I realized that I vaguely recognised her as someone I had gone to high-school with. She was a pretty enough woman, with a slender frame and a narrow waist underneath her knee-length skirt and blouse. Her dark hair was glossy and her makeup flawless, from her carefully shaped eyebrows to her pink lipstick traced with lip-liner that was just a shade darker, giving her mouth a fuller shape. Unfortunately, her impatient expression didn't match her good looks. I seemed to remember that she had always been pretty sour, even way back in school.

She approached the family and nodded towards the little girl.

"Make sure she doesn't touch anything, unless you're planning on buying it. I don't want all of my stock ruined with sticky handprints," Charlotte snapped.

The father looked taken aback by her outburst, but the mother, presumably a regular customer who knew Charlotte, replied quickly.

"She's not sticky, but don't worry. She won't be touching anything. Unlike some people, she has manners."

Charlotte glared at the woman and skulked off behind the counter. Yes, it seemed she was as unpleasant as Clayton.

The family moved away from Charlotte and went straight to a jungle gym. The man of the family picked up one of the large boxes, the woman took the little girl's hand, and they went to the counter with the box.

Charlotte's attitude changed within a second when she saw she was about to make a decent sale. It was funny how all of the Caldwells seemed not only to be mean, but also extremely greedy.

"Good choice," Charlotte said with a gleeful smile. She turned her beaming face to the little girl, no longer caring if she happened to have sticky hands. "Is this for you?"

The little girl hid behind her mom's legs and nodded mutely.

"You've just got this in time," Charlotte commented to the mom.

"Oh? Are you not going to carry them anymore?" the mom asked.

Charlotte shook her head and grinned. "Not just them. A family member died and left me an inheritance. Once I get it, I'll be closing this place and becoming a lady of leisure."

"I'm sorry to hear of your loss," the woman said.

Charlotte waved her apology away. "It's fine. I barely knew my great uncle. I'm just frustrated that my cousin is set to get a share too. What does he need with that kind of money? I've got much more right to it than he does. I'm contesting the will, of course. With any luck, he'll be cut out of it."

"Umm, congratulations," the woman replied awkwardly.

It was clear she had no idea what the appropriate response should be, but her congratulations seemed to work on Charlotte.

I thought that all Charlotte needed to do was rub her hands together and throw her head back and give a villainous laugh, and she'd make the perfect stereotypical villain.

Her talk of the inheritance she was set to receive made me think of Clayton again. Hadn't Mildred said he was about to inherit a large sum of money? He had to be the cousin Charlotte was talking about. He wasn't going to be happy when he learned she was trying to cheat him out of his share. If he didn't know already.

"Emma? Are you just going to stand there all evening, or are you actually going to help me?" Suzy asked.

I shook my head. I was getting drawn into the town gossip again. I grinned at Suzy and made my way over to her, no longer able to hear what Charlotte was saying to the family.

"I didn't think you needed any help." I laughed, nodding toward the armfuls of baby jumpers, vests and pajamas Suzy was clutching, as well as her ever growing list of nursery furniture.

Suzy dumped the armload of clothes on me.

"Of course I need help. Who else is going to convince Brian that all of this stuff is essential?"

As she talked, she put a packet of lion shaped pacifiers and a packet of muslin squares on the pile in my arms.

"You realize I'm not a miracle worker, right?" I asked.

Suzy picked up a tiny yellow hat and smiled. She held it up and I couldn't help but smile myself.

"See? How can you say this isn't essential?"

"Well, a hat that cute really is," I agreed.

Charlotte came over at that moment and I realized the other customers had left, probably glad to escape. I could imagine the family loading the jungle gym into the trunk of their car and laughing at Charlotte's change in demeanour. Probably discussing her despicable attitude toward her dead relative, too.

"Do you need any help?" Charlotte asked.

Her tone suggested she didn't much want to help us, but the dollar signs in her eyes meant she would do it all the same.

Suzy smiled politely and handed her the list. "You could order me all of these and arrange to have them delivered please," she said.

Charlotte's eyes lit up as she scanned the list. "Not a problem. Is it the same address as last time?"

Suzy nodded.

"Last time?" I probed.

"I already ordered a new stroller to be delivered at the house," Suzy informed me. "No one, not even Brian, can say a stroller isn't essential."

I had to give her that one. I was sure Brian hadn't objected to the baby having a stroller, but knowing Suzy's tastes, it probably would have been an overly expensive one.

Suzy led me by the arm back to the furniture section of the store and began pointing out what she was ordering. There was the bassinet of course, the white and yellow dresser, a matching wardrobe and a changing station adorned with little lilac colored hearts. There was also a baby bath and a changing mat that Suzy informed me was to stay downstairs in case of any "poonamis". The term made me wrinkle my nose and Suzy burst out laughing. Finally, she also added a nightlight.

"I've already ordered that," she said, pointing to a small, fluffy white rug. "I thought it would... Oh my goodness, Emma, look at that!"

She was practically running across the store and I followed her, grinning at her excitement. I remembered the time when she used to act like this in clothing stores, and then it was homeware stores. She definitely threw herself fully into whatever venture was on her mind. And whatever the venture was, shopping was always right at the heart of it.

She led me to a beautiful grey rocking horse. It was on mahogany runners and looked like an antique. It made me long to be a little kid again, just so I could ride it. It was the sort of rocking horse every little girl dreamed of owning, the one that would be the envy of all her friends.

"I have to get that, Emma. Right?" Suzy asked.

"What? No. You're having a baby, not a five year old," I replied.

Suzy frowned. "Have a bit of imagination, Emma. The baby will grow up, you know. And besides, it'll look so good in the nursery. I've already ordered a doll's house and a mahogany rocking chair to nurse in, so it'll fit right in. And let's think about this logically. If I wait until Aaron or Harley is five to buy the rocking horse, think how much more expensive it will be. By buying it now, I'm actually saving us money."

It was clear Suzy's mind was already made up. It had been from the moment she clapped eyes on the horse. And there was a certain twisted logic to her theory, although I wasn't so sure Brian would appreciate the hypothetical savings they had made. He'd accept it, though. He loved Suzy and would do whatever it took to make her happy. I got the impression his objections were just window dressing, that he was reacting the way he thought people would expect him to react to Suzy's spending of money they didn't really have on things they didn't really need.

"Who am I to stop little Aaron or Harley having the best toys ever?" I laughed. "But I really don't think I can convince Brian that's an essential."

"Essential schmential," Suzy said. "I'm getting it."

Charlotte was already hovering behind us with a sold sign in her hand. She was like the proverbial devil on Suzy's shoulder, enabling her craziness.

"Do you want it added to your delivery, or would you like it sent over tomorrow?" Charlotte asked, hooking the sign on the horse's neck and leaving Suzy no room to change her mind.

"You'd better send it with the rest so it can blend in a bit," Suzy said.

Charlotte snorted out a laugh that actually sounded genuine. Maybe she wasn't all bad, I thought to myself.

Suzy finally wandered over to the counter and I followed her across the shop and laid all of her other purchases near the cash register. I could feel my eyes watering when Charlotte announced her total. Suzy, unfazed, handed over a credit card.

"You could have paid for the kid's first year at college with that amount," I said.

Charlotte threw me a dirty look and I realized I was wrong – she was all bad. She obviously didn't know Suzy at all if she really thought my comment could sway her away from any of her purchases.

"What?" Suzy asked distractedly as she added a stuffed yellow duck and another tiny hat, this one mint green, to the pile.

"Nothing." I laughed.

Charlotte bagged up the things and handed them to

Suzy with a flourish. Suzy's eyes shone with excitement as she confirmed the delivery date for the furniture. As we left the shop, she looked longingly at the horse.

"I can't wait to get the nursery all set up," she said. "You and Billy will have to come by and see it when it's done. Brian is just finishing up the decorating. We've gone for white walls, and on the feature wall, Brian has painted the most adorable duckling scene."

"It sounds adorable. I'd love to come and take a look," I agreed, although I wasn't so sure Billy would view seeing a nursery as a fun night out.

We walked along the high street in the direction of Suzy's shop, loaded down with bags.

"Let's go dump these and then we'll grab some food, if you want. I'm starving," Suzy said.

I saw my chance to buy my underwear of shame in private. "I just have to grab something first. You go on ahead and I'll meet you at the Posh Closet," I said.

Suzy shook her head. "Nonsense. I don't mind carrying these bags a little longer. I'll come with you. What do you need?"

With a sinking heart, I pointed at the store I needed.

"Picking up something for your grandma?" Suzy asked.

I knew she wasn't even being sarcastic. Of course that's what she would think. It was the only reason I would enter a shop like this one. Except it wasn't.

"That's not it exactly," I confessed.

Suzy looked at me with a questioning frown. "Don't tell me being back here has gotten to you so much that you're going to start dressing like a character from another century even when you're not at the carnival?" she asked, incredulous.

I laughed. "No. But here's the deal. It's freezing in that

awful prairie dress Betty Blackwell is making me wear. And
the wind goes straight up the stupid skirt. So I want some
thermal underwear."

Suzy barked out a laugh as she pushed the door open. I
felt the blast of warmth from inside as we stepped in.

I quickly grabbed four pairs of thermal underwear, both
the long-sleeved tops and the bottoms with legs. If I was
going to do this, I may as well go all in and be nice and
warm. I paid for them before I could talk myself out of it.
When we left the store, I turned the carrier bag inside out so
no one would know my shameful shopping secret.

"This," I said, indicating the bag, "stays totally between
us. No telling anyone, not even Brian."

"Scouts honour," Suzy said, giving me a salute. "Now
let's go someplace where we can eat."

We slipped into a coffee shop that also served delicious
sandwiches and thick wedges of lemon pie that were to die
for. We spent the time huddled over the table talking about
Suzy's thoughts on motherhood and dissecting my relationship with Billy. I learned that Suzy was going to breastfeed
and that she was debating between home schooling the
little one, at least for the first few years, or sending them to
the school we both went to as kids. She learned that things
were going really well with Billy and me and that I wished
I'd listened to her when I first came back to town and had
gotten together with him straight away. It was always going
to happen. I had just been too darned stubborn to see it, at
first.

We left the restaurant, Suzy hugged me goodbye, and we
parted ways, both carrying off the bags full of our purchases.
As I headed back to the truck, I pictured Brian's face when
he saw all of the things Suzy had bought. It would be even

worse when their credit card bill came in. I couldn't help but smile at the thought of his jaw dropping and Suzy fluttering her eyelashes and acting all innocent, explaining that of course a rocking horse was essential for a newborn.

6

———

I got into the truck, started the engine, and waited a moment or two for the heat to kick in. Grandma had asked me to call by Hanson's Feed and Supplies and get some food for the chickens. I checked the time. I figured I would have enough time to get there and grab some chicken feed before they closed for the night. The various farm supply stores generally stayed open a little later than the other stores in town, as a lot of local farmers only managed to slip away for errands once the sun was setting and the farm had been kept in order for another day.

It was a vast difference from the big city, where all of the major stores were open late to catch the rush of workers finishing their jobs for the day and wanting to pop out shopping after changing and eating dinner. It still sometimes bothered me that everything closed so early here. Late night opening was considered to be eight p.m. in these parts. But I was slowly getting used to it, and I found the notion that if I didn't have something by eight I wouldn't have it until the next day made me a lot less materialistic. That had to be a good thing, I decided.

Once the cab heated up enough that I could just about feel my fingers again, I put the truck into drive and headed off in the direction of Hanson's Feed and Supplies. I'd been by with Grandpa enough times to know exactly where it was. I flicked the radio on as I drove and hummed along to the music. I yawned widely as I reached the road leading to the store. It had already been a long day and I would kill for an early night, but I knew I still had work to do when I got home.

I parked the truck and hopped down from the cab, once more assaulted by the cold air. The temperature was dropping fast as night settled in on the town. Even walking from the truck to the store, I kept my arms folded across my chest and my hands tucked into the warmth of my armpits. I was already craving summer and counting the days until the first daffodils of the season opened, indicating spring was on its way.

I pushed open the door of the large warehouse-style store and stepped inside. There were no other customers visible, but the door wasn't locked. I hoped that meant they were still open, rather than it being an oversight.

"Are you still open?" I asked the man behind the counter.

"Sure. We'll be open for another half an hour or so," he replied. He looked strangely nervous as he answered me.

"Oh, great. I just need to grab a bag of chickenfeed for my grandma," I said, walking further into the store.

He relaxed at my words. "That's good. Mr. Hanson will go crazy if he comes along to close up and I'm not ready. But he also goes crazy if I turn customers away. I can't seem to win with him," he said.

I laughed softly. "Sounds about right," I joked, thinking

of Betty Blackwell and how I too could never seem to win, no matter what I did.

I hurried through the maze of shelves, not wanting to get the young man into any trouble if Mr. Hanson arrived a little earlier than expected. I easily located the chickenfeed section and grabbed a bag of the familiar brand Grandma used. I lugged it back to the counter and paid.

"Thanks," I called over my shoulder as I left the store.

"Come again," the young man shouted back.

I loaded the chickenfeed into the truck bed and got back into the cab, pleased it was still a bit warm in there and I wouldn't have to sit and wait for it to heat up again. I drove back to the farm and unloaded the chickenfeed, leaving the offending thermals on the passenger seat for now.

I walked around the outside of the farmhouse, knowing Grandma wouldn't be happy if I trailed the bag of feed through the house. Feedbags always seemed to have a few loose grains stuck to the outside, which never fell until they were in the vicinity of carpet. I put the feed in the shed and entered the house via by the back door.

My grandparents sat at the kitchen table, eating supper. It was Grandma's famous minestrone soup and it smelled delicious but I was already stuffed full from my meal with Suzy.

"Do you want some? It's still warm," Grandma asked, standing up.

"No thank you," I said. "Sit back down. I had dinner with Suzy in town. That's why I'm a bit late."

I poured myself a cup of coffee and sat down with my grandparents.

"Your chickenfeed is in the shed," I said.

"Thanks, honey. How's Suzy and her bump? Is she getting plenty of rest?" Grandma asked.

"Suzy doesn't know the meaning of the word *rest*," I said. "But her and baby are both doing fine. We went to the Baby Boutique and picked out some furniture and more clothes than any infant could ever need, so I'm not sure how well Brian will be doing when he sees it all."

Grandma laughed. "He'll pretend to be annoyed, but deep down, he won't mind. He wants the best for the baby too. That's what it's like with your first one. You buy all the newfangled gadgets people say you can't live without, only to find you easily could have lived without them. Half of them never even make it out of the packaging and the stuff that does is never used enough to make buying it worthwhile. You buy all of the clothes in sight and the baby grows so fast they don't get to wear half of them. By the time she has another, she'll have learned and she'll only buy practical things that she actually needs – and most of those will be second hand."

"I hope so. Poor Brian won't know what's hit him if they go through all of this again." I laughed.

"Did you happen to see Sam Hanson when you picked up the chickenfeed?" Grandpa asked me.

I shook my head. "No. There was a young man at the check-out. He was expecting Sam to arrive around closing time, though. Why? Is he a friend of yours?"

Grandpa shrugged. "More of a business acquaintance really. I have a few things on order with him, that's all. I just wondered if he had mentioned their progress. Never mind, I can always pop over there one day, if I don't hear anything from him soon."

I finished my cup of coffee and went to the sink to wash it out. I started to fill the sink with warm soapy water to wash the rest of the dishes. Snowball appeared as I plunged my hands into the soapsuds, and my grandparents laughed when I tickled underneath her chin, leaving behind a beard of white suds.

As I washed the dishes, Grandma chatted away, telling me all of the gossip from her quilting group. I learned rather more than I ever wished to know about Diane's husband's gout. Grandma moved on to talk about her new book club, and I learned a lot about her friend Edie's fascination with the new cooking class she had joined.

"I'm thinking of going to it myself," Grandma said.

"A cooking class? Grandma, you could teach the teacher a thing or two about cooking," I said.

"She's right," Grandpa agreed. "These modern chefs, what do they know? Everything's always smothered in some sauce or other, and those portions wouldn't feed a baby."

Grandma laughed. "It was just an idea. I probably won't even end up going," she said.

Grandpa stood up and stretched and yawned. "Well, I reckon it's about time for me to turn in," he said.

Grandma nodded. "Yes, me too. Emma, you should have an early night too, while you have the chance."

"I will, Grandma," I said.

The truth was, I couldn't. I still had wood to collect and chop so it would be ready for tomorrow's fight with the wood burning stove. Then I had a graphic design project to finish up for a client. It was easier to agree with Grandma, though, than have her start worrying again that I was doing too much. Once I'd finished this project, if anything, I wouldn't have enough to do to fill my time.

My grandparents and I said our goodnights and each of them kissed my cheek. Then they were gone.

"Looks like it's just the two of us, Snowball," I said. "Fancy a little trip to the woodpile?"

As if she understood me, she went and stood at the

kitchen door. When I was too slow to follow her, she bleated impatiently and tapped her little horns against the door.

"Alright, alright, I'm coming." I laughed.

I opened the door and she rushed out into the night, a white blur in the darkness, her little tail bobbing up and down, matching her enthusiasm. I was slightly less enthusiastic as I made my way to the woodpile. My hands shook with the cold as I chopped the logs down to size and carried them into the kitchen. I took some time to arrange them properly inside the stove so that all I had to do tomorrow was get them burning.

I made a quick visit to the outhouse, again accompanied by Snowball, and then I locked the back door and headed through to the front of the house, where I slipped back out to the truck and gathered my shameful underwear. On my way in again, I almost tripped over Snowball, who had the good sense to wait for me inside the door rather than brave the elements further. It was just starting to drizzle outside as I closed and locked the front door.

I went through to the kitchen and made myself a big mug of sweet, hot cocoa and then I turned out the kitchen lights and headed upstairs, clutching my mug in one hand, and my carrier bag of underwear in the other. I wasn't so much hiding my purchases from my grandparents because I thought they'd tease me. It was more a case of knowing that if Grandma saw them, she'd insist on buying me more, and I had no intention of wearing them anywhere but at the carnival. I didn't much like being cold, but I had some standards and I refused to let being back in this small town turn me old before my time.

I was followed up to my attic bedroom by Snowball, who instantly hopped onto my bed and curled up in a tight little ball at the end of it.

I quickly changed into my pajamas and snuggled down under the duvet with my cocoa and my laptop. While I waited for my laptop to fire up, I sent Billy a quick text, telling him how much I was looking forward to our dinner tomorrow.

As I waited for a reply, I thought again of Betty saying the costume for the stall had been Beth's idea, and I tapped out a text to Beth.

ME: I can't believe U suggested a prairie dress to Betty for us to wear at the carnival. What were U thinking?

MY CELL PHONE vibrated and I checked the message. It was from Billy.

BILLY: I'm looking forward to it too. I miss you x.

I SMILED to myself and sent him a heart emoji. Then I went back to my laptop and opened up my client work. I began adding to the design, pleased with how it was coming together. When I'd almost given up on a reply from Beth, my cell phone buzzed again.

BETH: That sly old dog Betty told me it was your idea. She said we couldn't afford to rent a costume and asked me to make one. Said you'd be disappointed if I refused.

·   ·   ·

I COULDN'T HELP but laugh, shaking my head at Betty's cheek. It made much more sense that Betty was behind this, and I had to give her credit for the way she'd pulled off the ruse.

"Well played, Betty, well played," I said under my breath as I typed out a response to Beth.

ME: Haha. That makes much more sense. This is war.
BETH: It's so on.

I WENT BACK to my work and, when I finished the design, I sent it across for approval. By the time I was done, my eyelids were heavy, so I shut down my laptop and curled up under the covers, falling asleep almost instantly.

7

I had cheated a little bit this morning. When I woke up
at stupid o'clock, I was still so exhausted that I'd crept
out of bed and down the stairs and lit the wood
burner. Then I'd come back up and gotten back into bed to
grab a little extra sleep. I woke up two hours later feeling
much more refreshed and ready to face the day. It was still
an early morning by anyone's standards – well anyone who
didn't live on a farm – but to me, that extra sleep time felt
like a little luxury.

After I had showered and dressed, I went down to find
the house empty. I felt a moment of guilt. Grandpa and
Grandma were outside working while I had been sleeping
in. I reminded myself I'd completed my chores all the same
and my grandparents wouldn't care if I chose to have an
extra couple hours in bed rather than sitting at the kitchen
table. It helped ease the guilt, but didn't remove it entirely,
so I set about preparing breakfast, hoping that would make
up for it.

When breakfast was ready, I opened the back door and

called out to Grandma, who was in the chicken coop. She gave me a thumbs up and went off to find Grandpa. A couple of minutes later, the two of them arrived in the kitchen. Grandpa beamed when he saw the full meal spread out on the table. He began to load his plate as I made the coffee.

"Oh, Emma, you didn't have to do this," Grandma said as she helped herself to the food.

"I wanted to. It was no trouble," I said.

I handed out cups of coffee and sat down and filled my own plate, suddenly ravenous. The country air seemed to make me constantly hungry. It was probably a good thing I had chores to complete around the farm and was on the go with volunteer projects like the carnival. Otherwise, I was sure I would have been about five lbs heavier than I had been when I'd first returned to Hillbilly Hollow.

We all tucked into our breakfasts. Grandpa nodded appreciatively as he chewed and I felt a moment of relief that my breakfast was passing his taste test.

"What are your plans for today, Emma?" Grandma asked.

"I'm back at the carnival until four, then I'm meeting up with Billy for dinner," I said.

Grandma smiled knowingly. "Lovely boy is Billy," she said.

"Yes. He is," I agreed.

She winked. "I hear talk he's no longer available."

I felt my cheeks flush pink and I laughed quietly. "He must be making some girl very happy."

"That he is, judging by the flush in her cheeks," Grandma grinned.

"Do you two do anything but gossip? Let the doctor be,

he deserves a good wife," Grandpa said, still oblivious to the fact that the woman Billy was dating was me.

"He does. And he'll get one, if he treats this new girl-friend right," Grandma commented.

Grandpa rolled his eyes and buttered a slice of toast.

I finished eating and stood up. "I hate to dine and dash, but I really should go and get ready. Leave the pots and I'll do them tonight."

"You cooked, the least we can do is clean the dishes," Grandpa said.

"Plus, think how disgusting they'd be if we left them out all day," Grandma added, wrinkling her nose.

I smiled as I left the room and went back up to the attic. As I bundled myself into my awful underwear, I couldn't help but smile at how warm it made me feel. I quickly threw my jeans back on and added a thick sweater to my top half. I'd have preferred to look nicer for my date this evening, but I figured a sweater was better than a strappy top over freez-ing, blue flesh.

When I came back downstairs, I found Snowball in the kitchen, eating a sausage. I said goodbye to my grandparents and made my way out to the truck. The day was as bitingly cold as yesterday, but I felt a whole lot warmer. As I drove toward the carnival grounds, I found myself thinking about Billy. I was whistling a happy tune by the time I arrived at the parking lot.

I was shocked at how busy the parking lot was already. It looked like the carnival was going to be more of a success than any of us had imagined. I was still whistling as I cut the engine and hopped down from the truck.

Nearby, a young woman named Jemima Cole was lingering in the lot. At the noise of my truck door slamming, she glanced in my direction and shook her head. I knew her vaguely as the plump, pretty blond who worked at the hotdog stand near my kettle corn booth. I'd noticed before that she always seemed to be in a bad mood, but today her expression was grumpy, even for her.

"Can't you show some respect?" she snapped.

I was taken aback by the glare and her words, and I had no idea what she was talking about. She must have seen by the look on my face how confused I was. Her expression softened and she shook her head.

"Never mind. You obviously didn't know," she said.

I moved a bit closer to her, my curiosity piqued now.

"Didn't know what? What's going on?" I asked.

Jemima said, "Everyone is saying that a dead body was found in this parking lot. An early morning dog walker discovered it and called for Sheriff Tucker."

I gasped. "That's awful!"

Jemima nodded. "Yep. They're still waiting for an ambulance to come and collect the body."

She didn't have to explain why the ambulance would have been delayed in arriving. Everyone knew Hillbilly Hollow was too small to merit its own hospital. All we had was our little clinic, where Billy worked, and a separate doctor's office on the opposite side of town that mostly focused on elderly patients. When there was a real emergency, an ambulance had to be sent from the next town over.

"What do they think happened?" I asked.

"No idea, but I hear there was lots of blood. You wouldn't see that if the man just dropped dead of his own accord, would you? And why would someone even be in the parking lot in the middle of the night?"

"The middle of the night?" I repeated.

Jemima nodded, her eyes lighting up as she got to impart the next bit of gruesome information.

"Word is, by the time he was found, his body was frozen solid. I reckon he must have been out here quite some time for that to happen. Wouldn't you agree?"

I nodded absently, my focus no longer on Jemima. I began to ease my way through a crowd that I now realized wasn't just here for the carnival. They were onlookers at what might be a crime scene. I looked for Tucker, wanting to find out exactly what had happened and what it meant for the carnival. I thought of the light in Jemima's eyes as she had told me the story, and I couldn't help but think it was a bit hypocritical for someone who had called me disrespectful for whistling and slamming a door to take such relish in passing on the gory details of some poor man's death.

As I made my way through the crowd, I caught bits of conversation here and there.

"What's the doctor here for? I think he's past needing a doctor."

"This town is turning into the murder capital of the country."

"Scary, isn't it?"

"The guy probably had a heart attack or something, but none of these vultures will leave him in peace."

Another hypocrite, I thought as I heard that last comment. I didn't see any of these people exactly hurrying to get out of the way. By the snippet about the doctor being here, I figured Tucker must have called in Billy. It would indeed be too late for him to do anything, but a doctor had to be present in the event of a death, and as Billy was the nearest one, he often got called out to do the unpleasant task of officially pronouncing a person dead.

I had made my way halfway across the parking lot when I heard sirens in the distance. As they quickly grew closer, the crowd reluctantly parted to let the ambulance in. The vehicle pulled up, lights flashing, and I edged closer as two paramedics alighted. I tore my eyes from the emergency workers to look around the scene. Through the sea of heads in my way, I could make out the figures of Sheriff Tucker and a couple of his deputies.

My eyes snagged on Billy's tall, dark frame, standing with Tucker. I was too far away to hear what was being said, but I saw Billy talking to the sheriff and greeting the paramedics as they pushed through the crowd. One of the paramedics briefly conferred with Billy, while another opened up the back doors of the ambulance and pulled out a stretcher.

They moved the stretcher through the gathering until they reached the spot where the dead man was lying on the pavement inside a chalk outline. With so many onlookers blocking my view, I couldn't see the body itself clearly until they bent down and lifted it. When they straightened back up and placed the corpse on the stretcher, one of them quickly draped a sheet over the still form. But not before I glimpsed a flash of bright orange sweater.

For an instant, my heart seemed to stand still in my chest. I knew that sweater, I realized, stunned. Not only that, but I knew the lifeless figure wearing it. The dead man was none other than Clayton Caldwell.

I felt a strange mixture of emotions on discovering the identity of the dead man. Relief that it was no one I knew well, followed by guilt, because it was wrong to be relieved. Clayton might have been an unpleasant person, but it was tragic when anyone died.

The paramedics finished loading the stretcher into the

ambulance, then they clambered inside and the engine roared to life. Even though the sirens remained silent this time, people moved to let them through. A couple of men in the crowd removed their hats and bowed their heads as the ambulance left the scene.

Now that the show was over, the crowd began to thin almost instantly, and I was easily able to get close enough to overhear Tucker and Billy talking about Clayton's untimely demise.

"So in your opinion, he'd been dead for some time?" Tucker asked.

"I would say he died around four to six hours ago. Of course, the temperature last night would have sped up the rigor mortis, but the body wasn't fresh. The bleeding had stopped long ago," Billy said.

I could hear a note of irritation in Billy's voice, so I suspected this was the third or fourth time he had explained this to Tucker.

Tucker scribbled away on a form as Billy talked.

"The cause of death was obviously the bullet wound to the back. The autopsy report will confirm the exact injury, but I'd be surprised if it was down to anything but the bullet penetrating the liver," Billy said.

Bullet? Clayton had been shot? And in the back? It struck me as a rather cowardly way to kill someone. Even someone like Clayton Caldwell deserved the respect to at least look him in the eye before you pulled the trigger.

"Judging from the shape and size of the wound, it looks like the shooter was some distance away from the victim. If he had been shot at close range, there would have been a large exit wound. But as you saw, the bullet remained embedded in the body, which suggests the force wasn't enough for the shooter to have been close," Billy said. His voice changed slightly, losing the professional tone. "He probably didn't even see it coming. He would have had a split second from hearing the gun go off before the bullet penetrated him. Not even enough time to turn around."

"Yes, it's a terrible shame isn't it," Tucker said. "Makes you wonder what's wrong with some people."

"I just can't fathom why he was even here at such an odd hour unless there is a reason we're missing. If that's the case, and I suspect it is, then we're not looking at a spur of the moment thing. We're looking at a pre-meditated homicide," Billy mused.

"Let's not be hasty now," Tucker cautioned. "There's every possibility that he was just early for the carnival opening and decided to hang around here in the parking lot until it opened up for the day. This could be a random mugging gone wrong."

I was surprised at the weakness of Tucker's theory. Who turned up in the middle of the night for a carnival opening? And then decided to just wait there?

"Really? Do you think that's very likely?" I heard Billy ask, as if trying to keep the surprise from his voice.

Tucker shrugged. "It's possible," he said, somewhat defensively.

"Right, of course," Billy said. "Look, I have to get back to the clinic. If you need any help translating the autopsy report when it comes in, give me a call."

"Thanks doc," Tucker said.

I considered going after Billy, who headed off without ever seeing me. But instead, I chose to hang around the parking lot for a moment longer. It wouldn't hurt to do a quick check of the area. And if what I'd heard was the best theory Tucker had, then he was going to need any help he could get. I was inclined to think Billy's suggestion was right. Clayton had been lured here and then murdered.

I looked at the chalk outline where the body had been lying. If the victim had been shot in the back, he would have fallen forwards and landed face-down, so the position of the body suggested the shot had to have come from the direction of the carnival. That made sense. The carnival's fence would have cast a thick enough shadow for the gunman to hide in if no one was looking closely. And if Clayton thought he was meeting someone, it made sense that he would be facing out into the parking lot, rather than looking toward the carnival itself.

I set off in that direction. I hadn't gone far when something lying between the painted stripes of a couple empty parking spaces caught my eye. I crouched down to look. It was a medium-sized pink button. It was an unusual shape for a button—square. I straightened and waved at Tucker.

He spotted me and waved his hand in return. I beckoned to him and he came closer.

"Terrible business, isn't it?" he said by way of a greeting.

He pushed his hat to the back of his head and scratched at his blond beard. His handsome face was drawn into its usual grave expression that always had a hint of confusion about it, as if even he was unsure how he had come to be in his position as sheriff of Hillbilly Hollow.

"Shocking," I agreed. I pointed down at the button. "Look. This could have come from the shooter's clothing. It certainly didn't come from Clayton's."

Used to my nosey ways, Tucker didn't even ask how I knew who the victim was or how I was so sure the button wasn't Clayton's. He had learned by now that I often pried into criminal situations and that, more often than not, my prying turned out to be useful.

He bent down and peered at the button as though waiting for it to spill all of its owner's secrets. Then he pulled a clear baggie from his pocket and bagged the tiny item.

"I'll send this over to the forensics lab if you've got a feeling about it, but I'm not holding out much hope of getting anything useful from it," he said. "The parking lot has been teeming with people this morning, and think how much foot traffic there was here yesterday for the carnival."

I knew he was right. The parking lot had been busy these past couple of days and had collected plenty of trash and debris. Realistically, the button could've come from anyone. There was no indication it had belonged to the murderer, other than my hunch. But right now the button was all we had to go on, and it was something, which had to be better than nothing.

I said goodbye to Tucker and walked away, my mind whirling. I wished I had taken a picture of the button so I knew exactly what it looked like, but I was sure if I saw a matching set, especially on a sweater with one missing, I would recognise it.

It looked like the sort of button you would find on the type of cardigan older ladies often wore. But what old lady would be running around in the middle of the night with a gun? One who had something serious against Clayton Caldwell, that much was clear.

That made me think of Mildred, Clayton's assistant in the bookstore. She'd been wearing a pink cardigan the last time I saw her, hadn't she? And she'd made no secret of her intense dislike for Clayton, especially as she suspected he was planning on selling her very home out from under her.

Mildred had motive for sure. And maybe the mystery man I had seen Clayton arguing with in the parking lot yesterday evening had motive too.

Something told me I wasn't going to rest until I learned the truth about what had happened here last night.

8

I had barely gotten my costume on and emerged from behind the changing screen when Tucker burst into the marquee.

"Who's in charge here?" he demanded.

Betty Blackwell stepped forward from behind her desk.

"The town council organised the carnival, Sheriff, but the chairman isn't here right now. Can I be of any assistance?"

I had to lower my head to hide my smile. Betty would be loving life now that she was getting to pretend to be in charge of, not just the kettle corn stand, but the whole carnival. No one else in the marquee contradicted her, either. No one but Betty would want the extra work that could come with such an admission.

"I assume you heard about what happened in the parking lot?" Tucker asked Betty.

She nodded. "Yes. I think it was inconsiderate of the killer to carry out his terrible act in such a public place. Don't you?"

Tucker stared, as if not knowing how to answer the question.

Betty didn't seem to mind not getting any answer. "What do you need here, Sheriff?" she asked.

"A forensics team will be here as quickly as they can. In the meantime, I need to cordon off the broader area, and I'm afraid that means the carnival's opening today will have to be delayed until I can arrange things."

"You can rely on me to get that message out, of course," Betty said. "But I have to say this is all a most inconvenient and disappointing turn of events. I really feel like murder and carnivals shouldn't mix."

She tried to sound irritated, but I could hear the pride in her voice that she had been chosen to make sure the carnival was kept closed until Tucker gave the word. She had, it seemed, conveniently forgotten that she had volunteered herself for this, rather than being chosen.

Tucker nodded his thanks, ignoring her comments about murder being inconvenient, and left the marquee.

Betty turned to me. "Emma, a lot of the stall holders are already out in the grounds setting up. Can you be a dear and go around to inform them all of the delayed opening so they don't start cooking anything just yet?"

I nodded my agreement. With my new underwear, the marquee felt too warm and I would rather wander around the carnival than be stuck in here listening to Betty moan about how unacceptable this whole murder business was.

9

A few hours later, I checked my watch again and was relieved to see it was almost ten to four. It had taken Tucker a long time to get all his arrangements underway before finally declaring that the carnival could open.

The late start coupled with talk of a murder in the parking lot must have put off a lot of potential visitors, because now the carnival was so quiet it was ridiculous. The rides barely moved and the atmosphere was one of silent reflection rather than the usual excitement.

No laughter or screams of delight filled the air and I had barely sold any kettle corn. The day had dragged by so slowly I felt as though time had actually stopped, at one point. I was a little surprised that more residents hadn't turned out just to see the scene of the crime and have a gossip. I decided most of them who turned out for that sort of thing had probably already gawked at the crime scene from a distance and then wandered across the road to the coffee shop or the nearest restaurant to discuss their theories on it, rather than coming to the carnival. Those with young children had probably opted to stay away.

I hoped it was only a one day lull and that the murder wouldn't cast a pall over the whole carnival. I chastised myself for thinking that way. It was too close to Betty's selfish reaction for my liking.

Speak of the devil, I thought as I spotted Betty heading towards me.

"Norma is taking over from you, Emma. You need to go and change so she can have the dress. I'll mind the stall in the meantime," she said.

I smiled sweetly and handed her my bonnet. "You should put this on until Norma gets here, just to keep the feel of the time going," I said.

She looked ready to argue, but I guessed she knew that if she did, she wouldn't have a leg to stand on to make any of the rest of us wear the costume. With a fake smile, she snatched the bonnet from me and jammed it onto her head.

"Adorable," I said.

I turned and walked away before my smile could turn into a laugh. I hurried back to the marquee and changed out of my dress, removing my underwear of shame and stuffing them into my bag in the process. When I was dressed in my normal clothes again, I stepped out from behind the screen.

"All yours," I told Norma, the middle-aged volunteer waiting for her turn. "Betty has the bonnet."

"You got her to wear it?" Norma asked, a look of shock crossing her face. Her blond eyebrows climbed all the way up to her mismatched red hair.

"Yup." I laughed. "I told her she should wear it, just to keep the feel of the stall correct for the times."

"Oh, Emma, you're so bad." Norma laughed as she took the dress and went behind the screen.

I hurried through the carnival and checked my watch. I wouldn't have time to get home and shower and change before I was due to be at Billy's place, so I decided to just head over there now instead. He wouldn't mind if I was a little early, I figured.

I drove over to his place and parked in the driveway. I took a few minutes to apply a fresh layer of lip gloss and run a comb through my hair. Then I jumped down from the truck and headed to Billy's door.

Billy answered the door seconds after I rang the bell. He beamed when he saw me and gestured for me to come in.

I always enjoyed entering Billy's house, and not just because of Billy himself. It was a beautiful place, easily one of the nicest in town, and Billy had done a lot of the renovations himself, including adding a deck out back and putting new fixtures and flooring into the kitchen and bathrooms. The furnishings and decoration were tasteful too, right down to the black and white photos hanging in thick frames on the walls.

Billy turned to me and kissed my right cheek and then my left one. He laughed a little self-consciously, and then kissed my lips too. After he took my coat, he ushered me through to the living room.

"It's going to be about half an hour before dinner is ready. Would you like a glass of wine while we wait?"

"I'd love one." I smiled.

He headed for the kitchen and as the door opened I smelled the delicious aroma coming from inside. My stomach growled at the smell.

"What are we having?" I called through to the kitchen as I heard the clinking of the wine glasses.

Billy appeared back in the living room with two large glasses of white wine.

"Chicken Alfredo," he said. "Is that okay?"

"It's perfect," I told him.

He handed me one of the glasses of wine and raised his own, clinking it delicately against mine.

"Cheers," he said.

"Cheers," I repeated, before taking a sip of the cool, crisp wine.

"Did business at the carnival suffer today?" Billy asked, sitting down on the couch beside me. "I'm guessing you've heard by now about what happened in the parking lot?"

"Yeah, it was the talk of the place. And business was really quiet," I said. "Do you know it took Tucker two hours just to get the crime scene cordoned off? By then, there's no telling how many people had already gone traipsing through the parking lot, potentially ruining evidence."

Billy shook his head. "The man has interesting methods, doesn't he?" he said.

I laughed softly at his calling Tucker's disorganized approach a method. I said, "I was there earlier when you were talking to him. Your face was an open book when he suggested Clayton had arrived for the carnival in the middle of the night and had just decided to wait there for it to open. You didn't believe it."

"It seems far-fetched to me," Billy admitted.

The conversation moved on to lighter topics and Billy told me about his day. I told him about getting Betty to wear the bonnet and he laughed so hard wine came out his nose, which only made him laugh harder.

He had just about gotten himself back under control when a pinging noise sounded from the kitchen. He stood up.

"That's the oven timer. Do you want to go on through to the dining room?" he asked.

I went to the table, smiling at the candle Billy had placed in the centre. He brought the chicken into the kitchen and served us each a nice big portion. I waited until he took his seat before I tasted the chicken. It was cooked to perfection.

"Oh, wow. That's amazing," I said. "You know, for the rest of our lives you're officially in charge of all the cooking."

I could have bitten my tongue as soon as I said the words. Had I really just implied we'd be together for the rest of our lives, when we'd only been dating a few weeks?

If Billy noticed my embarrassing slip-up, he didn't comment on it. "Deal," he said. "As long as mowing the lawn is your thing. Coming from a farm, that's got to be a speciality of yours."

"That works for me." I laughed.

"Do you ever think about the future, Emma? Like, in a serious way?" he asked, suddenly earnest.

Uh-oh. Maybe he had noticed after all.

I nodded cautiously. "Sure," I said.

"Me too. And I just want you to know that when I picture the future, you're in it."

I felt the color rise in my cheeks, but it was with pleasure rather than embarrassment. When I thought of my future, he was very much a part of it too. But I had a secret, and I knew if we were really going to make this thing work between us, that he had a right to know about it. I hadn't planned on telling him so soon, but I felt like if I didn't say anything now, it would be akin to lying to him and I didn't want to start things out that way.

"You've gone quiet," Billy said. "I hope I haven't come on too strong and scared you."

I shook my head. "No, of course not. I was just thinking. Listen, there's something I have to tell you and I'm not sure what you're going to make of it."

"Whatever it is, we'll work it out together," he said. But his smile slipped a little and I could see concern in his eyes.

I nodded my head. I knew he meant that, but I wasn't so sure he was ready for what I was about to tell him. He was probably waiting for me to say I had commitment issues or something. He wouldn't be expecting what I was really going to confess. It would take someone extremely open minded to accept the truth of my next words.

I was about to tell him about the ghosts that visited me. He already knew I had an uncanny knack of getting mixed up in ongoing murder investigations, but the fact that I solved cases before Tucker did probably didn't strike Billy as that odd, knowing Tucker as he did. Billy also knew I saw ghosts. Only he didn't know they were *real* ghosts. He believed I had hallucinations brought on by a head injury I'd suffered in the accident that had led me back to Missouri. The truth was, I had let him believe that because it was easier than trying to explain that, actually, they weren't hallucinations. They were real.

But if we were going to be together, he had to know the truth, because it was a big part of who I was.

"Do you remember when I first came back to town and I told you about the accident I'd been in and the visions I was having?" I started.

Billy nodded. "Yes, of course. Emma, I'm a doctor. I understand hallucinations and they don't scare me, if that's what you're worried about," he said gently.

"It's not that," I said. "But the hallucinations, as you call them... Billy they aren't hallucinations. I truly see the ghosts of people with unfinished business, murder victims who can't move on until they have justice. I know how crazy that sounds, believe me I do, but I also know this is real. It's something that apparently runs in my family. Whenever I see one of these spirits, I'm compelled to do their bidding and help them find peace, so they can move on. That's why I always seem to end up doing amateur sleuthing. Because the dead people ask me to."

After spilling so many words in a rush, I finally fell silent, waiting for Billy's reaction.

He didn't speak at first. He kept his eyes on the shiny surface of the table instead of on me. As the awkward silence stretched on, I sensed it had been a mistake opening up to him. He looked extremely uncomfortable, as if he was sitting there thinking of how to break the news to me that I was insane.

"Billy?" I prompted after the quiet dragged on too long. "Please say something."

"I don't really know what to say, Emma. It's hard for me to accept that what you're seeing is anything other than a long-term medical side effect of a bang on the head."

"Just because something can't be explained by science doesn't make it untrue," I said, speaking more defensively than I'd meant to.

"Yes, you're right," Billy agreed, but his tone said the opposite of his words. He finally met my gaze. "But whatever these – these *ghosts* ask, I want you to promise me you won't do the type of investigating that puts you into danger, that you'll always work from a safe distance."

Every instinct in me was screaming to just agree that I would play it safe. But I'd already made up my mind to put my cards on the table and I wasn't going to tell him the hard part and then lie now.

"I can't always do that," I replied. "I mean, I won't take needless risks, but I have to leave no stone unturned to get at the truth. These spirits have no one else to speak up for them or act on their behalf. And if getting that justice for them sometimes puts me in danger, then it's a risk I'm willing to take."

Billy's lips tightened into a flat line, but he didn't argue with me. Instead, he stood up and changed the subject abruptly. "I'll get dessert," he announced as he left the room.

We ate the warm apple pie he brought back in an awkward silence. After dinner, we moved back to the living room, where the atmosphere became a little less strained as we made small talk about safe topics. But it still wasn't as easy as it usually was between us. When I feigned a yawn and said I was tired, Billy seemed only too willing to let me leave early.

As I drove back to the farm, I couldn't help thinking that I had destroyed any chance we had of making our romance work. I tried to tell myself that if Billy couldn't accept me for who I was, every part of me, then he was never the one for me anyway. But the thought did nothing to ease the hurt I felt when I realized I had most likely lost him for good.

10

I forced myself to put Billy and the secret I should never have spilled out of my mind, while I followed Grandpa around the fields that evening, holding a variety of nails and a hammer as he double-checked all of the pens and fences. He tut-tutted to himself now and again as we walked, and sometimes he shook his head in obvious annoyance, although he didn't share with me what he was annoyed about.

We reached a gate and he shook his head again, scratching the top of it, as he peered at the latch. This time, he stopped walking and bent down for a closer look. I peered over his shoulder, but I could see nothing that should have irritated him so much.

"What is it?" I asked, seeing no fault with the latch.

Grandpa pointed and I leaned down and looked closer.

"See here? The cows have been kicking at the gate again. They've loosened the latch. Another couple of kicks and the gate could've come clean off. Then we'd have cows everywhere and would have to round up the whole herd before they took off down the road."

He reached for the hammer and I smiled to myself.

"What's so funny?" he asked.

"Nothing. I just couldn't help but picture the whole farm overrun by escaped cows with you chasing behind them, shouting at them to get back into their field. And then I pictured one making its way into the kitchen and Grandma refusing to send it away, making it a housepet, like she did with Snowball."

Snowball bleated from beside me as I said her name, no doubt annoyed at the idea of any other creature stealing part of her limelight.

Grandpa laughed. "Now don't you go telling your grandma that. She would love the idea of a pet cow. In fact, she would probably want to come out here and handpick one to move in with us." He waggled his finger playfully at me. "And don't pretend you wouldn't back her up and add to your collection of furry shadows."

He nodded toward Snowball, who bleated again.

As Grandpa selected a nail and began hammering it into the gatepost, I crouched down and rubbed the little white goat behind her ears.

I said, "You don't have to be jealous, Snowball, I only have eyes for you. There'll be no pet cows for me."

"That should hold it," Grandpa said, standing back and admiring his handiwork.

I held my hand out for the hammer, but he shook his head. "That's enough for today. I'll finish up tomorrow. I have a few bits to do inside the house now. You should come inside too. It's freezing out here and it's getting dark," he said.

I nodded and handed him the remaining nails. "I'll be along in a bit. I just want to get some extra firewood chopped while there's still enough light. It's so much easier having it done in advance than trying to cut it in the middle of the night."

Grandpa snorted a laugh. "Middle of the night indeed. By the time you come down to light the stove, it's not night, it's morning."

"Maybe for you it is. But trust me, for the rest of the world it's very firmly the middle of the night." I laughed.

"The rest of the world are missing out," he said. "Early morning is the most peaceful and productive time to get things done with no distractions."

I didn't bother to point out to him that in the city where I used to live there would be distractions regardless of the time. It was true what they said about the city never sleeping. There was always something going on even in the dead of night, and if you were looking for a distraction you could easily find one.

Grandpa and I headed back in the direction of the house with Snowball happily trotting along between us.

"Well, this is where we part ways." I grinned as I turned off and headed for the woodshed, while Grandpa continued on towards the house.

Snowball followed Grandpa a few steps and then she looked to her side, searching for me. She bleated in alarm, stopping dead and turning around, an almost human expression of confusion on her little face when she realized I wasn't beside her.

Spotting me, she ran towards me, her bleats sounding angrier now, like she was annoyed that I had left her. Maybe she thought I was trying to trick her so I could ditch her and trade her in for a cow. Grandpa and I looked at each other and laughed at her indignation. When she reached my side, she made a snorting noise.

"I'm sorry, girl," I said. "I thought maybe you wanted to go inside where it's warm."

"You mean where your grandma will feed her," Grandpa shouted after me and we both laughed again at the truth of his statement.

I made my way to the woodshed and went in. It was every bit as cold in there as it was outside, but within a few minutes of hauling and chopping the wood, I was more than warm enough. Sweat covered me and I debated taking my coat off, but I didn't want to lose the rhythm I had built up and slow myself down. I reached up with one hand and wiped the sweat from my brow, then went on chopping.

As I worked, Billy's face swam into my mind, and I wondered again if I had lost him for good, not just as a romantic partner but as a friend. I had known he would find my secret hard to accept; he was a man of science. But I had hoped he would at least be willing to discuss it further. The way he had gotten up and ran for dessert, though, told me he wasn't open to thinking I could be right.

I brought the axe down in a particularly hard swing as my anger at him surfaced. How could he just dismiss my words so easily, after we had been friends for so long? It wasn't as if I had ever been one to be taken by flights of fancy.

Once more I told myself it was done now. If he couldn't accept what I was, rather than what he wanted me to be, then nothing would ever have worked with us anyway. It was better to know that now, instead of a year or two down the line. Still, the thought did nothing to ease the pain I felt. Neither did the anger, which I suspected was more of a cover for how sad losing him made me, rather than real anger.

"Oh, Snowball, should I have just kept quiet about it all? Should I have kept my secret?" I asked her.

Maybe I should have. Maybe there were some things that were best left unsaid, even between couples. My grandparents had their secrets from each other, and look at them. They were happy. Did it hurt either of them not knowing that the other used a secret trick to light up the wood burning stove? No. Did it hurt Grandma to not know that sometimes she had funny turns that Grandpa had learned to deal with? No. But it would perhaps hurt her if she did know the truth. Just like my truth had hurt my relationship with Billy when my silence could have saved it. Maybe I was naïve for not wanting a relationship filled with secrets. Maybe I would never meet anyone who could accept my strange habit of seeing ghosts. If Billy, someone who had known me forever, couldn't accept it, then who could?

Snowball's bleat in response to my question didn't give me any answers, but I felt as though her doleful brown eyes at least contained a modicum of sympathy for my plight. More likely she was wishing I would hurry up so we could get into the warmth of the house, but a girl could console herself by believing her pet goat felt her pain, right?

That sentence was crazy enough to make me smile despite myself. I would get through this. I'd gotten through worse. And maybe one day Billy would come around and we could at least be friends again. Or maybe he wouldn't, and I would have to learn how to live my life without him in it. Either way, I would survive. Continuing to think about it now wasn't doing anything to help me, so I vowed to let the matter rest for a while.

I finished chopping the wood and left the shed. The chill air immediately wrapped itself around me, turning the layer of sweat on my face cold. I shivered as I walked. Through the gathering gloom, I saw Grandpa's tall figure hurrying in my direction as I headed towards the house.

"Grandpa, what are you doing back out here?" I called to him.

"I'm not your grandpa. Shut up and listen," the man snapped, as he closed the distance between us.

I started, realizing I had been mistaken. The figure approaching me through the shadows was vaguely familiar but now I realized he was too wavering and indistinct to be my grandpa or any other living being. He was, in fact, a ghost. The ghost of Clayton Caldwell. I should have known it. I had been waiting for him to turn up, and the brusque manner and rudeness of his greeting should have tipped me off.

"You need to find the person who did this to me," he ordered, coming to a stop in front of me.

I was less surprised by his arrival—ghosts were common enough in my life—than by his demanding approach. I took a deep breath, willing myself to be civil with him, although even in death he didn't bother to extend the same courtesy to me. Who would come to ask for someone's help with that attitude?

"What happened, Mr. Caldwell? Did you see anyone before you were shot?" I asked hopefully.

"No. Whoever it was, they were too much of a coward for that. They came at me from behind. I need you to fix this. The killer needs to pay!"

With that, he was gone, his flickering form vanishing from sight right in front of my eyes. I blinked, wanting to be sure he had definitely gone and I hadn't just imagined him disappearing.

"Such a charming man. Dying clearly hasn't mellowed him," I said to myself as I started walking again.

I had expected the visit. It seemed every spirit in town was able to come and find me whenever it suited them. I should have expected the attitude, but somehow I hadn't. Maybe I had thought death would soften him a little. But if anything, it had only served to make him angrier and more bitter.

He didn't seem to have any interest in moving on. He was extremely vengeful and seemed to only want to know who had killed him so he could have the last laugh. It worried me a bit, but not enough that I would refuse him help. I had pretty much already decided I was going to look into his murder the moment I had heard Tucker's ridiculous theory about his death being unpremeditated.

Someone had to solve the crime, not for revenge, but for the safety of all the other citizens in town, who didn't deserve to live with a murderer wandering free in their midst.

11

___

The following morning, as I finished my chores around the farm, I couldn't stop my mind from going back to my ghostly visitor from last night. Although his attitude irked me, I knew I still had to investigate the murder.

And I had a good idea who to start with. Mildred Benson.

Although she seemed like a lovely, sweet old woman, sometimes appearances could be deceptive, and she had a perfect motive for wanting Clayton Caldwell dead. Maybe the stress of knowing she stood to lose her job and her home in one fell swoop had pushed her over the edge. Or maybe Clayton was horrible to her one time too many and she just snapped and decided to end his life. Stranger things had happened.

The square button I had found at the crime scene certainly brought her and her pink cardigan to mind. In fact, the more I pictured the button, the more I convinced myself it matched the ones on her cardigan the day I was in the bookstore. I knew I had to go back there and sniff around a little bit to see if I could spot anything unusual. Maybe I would even be lucky enough to get a look at the cardigan with its missing button. That was probably more than I could hope for, but it would make my job so much easier if it actually happened.

I called out my goodbyes to my grandparents and bent down to scratch Snowball underneath her chin before I left for the day. I had to be at the carnival in an hour, and I knew that would give me enough time to go to the bookstore first.

Anyway, if I arrived too early at my kettle corn stand, then what would Betty Blackwell have to gripe me out over? I would hate to deny her the pleasure of having something to moan about.

"Wish me luck, girl," I whispered to Snowball as I straightened and headed for the front door, making sure the little goat wasn't trying to follow me out into the yard.

When she bleated in response, I grinned. Snowball thought I would find something at the bookstore too.

Outside, I climbed into the truck and drove back over to the bookstore. I parked in the same place I had the last time I'd visited and made the short walk to the shop. As I was almost there, it suddenly hit me that the store would likely be closed. But since I was so close, I decided to check it out anyway.

To my surprise, when I arrived at the door I found the sign in the window turned to *open*. I shrugged and pushed through the door, hearing the tinkling sound of the bell ringing as I entered.

Mildred Benson stood behind the counter. She smiled at me as I came inside.

"Back so soon? Did your friend like the book you got her the other day?"

"Oh, she loved it. In fact, I'm here to look for another

book." I smiled, a little surprised that Mildred remembered my reason for buying Suzy's book. Was it a sign of good customer relations from someone who enjoyed her job, or was it a way of letting me know she was suspicious of my motives for being back at the store so soon?

She stepped around the counter, still smiling, and I saw she was wearing the same pink cardigan she'd had on last time. I subtly scanned my eyes up and down it. None of her buttons were missing, but they did look very similar to the square one I had spotted in the carnival's parking lot. I couldn't help but wonder if she had another cardigan just like this, one she had replaced after it had lost its button.

I shook my head. Was I really suspecting sweet little Mildred of a murder?

"Are you alright, dear?" Mildred asked, giving me a look of concern and stepping a little closer.

My sense of guilt increased as she showed concern for me, even while I had been thinking terrible things about her. I tried to swallow my suspicions, but the idea that she could have another, identical cardigan wouldn't leave my head, and the more I tried to ignore my thoughts, the more they screamed at me, reminding me that Mildred had the perfect motive for killing Clayton. Her kindness could be an act, I told myself.

I wondered vaguely whether this town and my recent investigations here had made me more alert and receptive to the nuances of human nature than I used to be. Or maybe I was just growing more cynical. Either way, I had to stop over-thinking this and just get on with the reason I was here.

I forced myself to focus on Mildred.

"I'm fine, thank you," I said.

My voice came out a little shaky, and Mildred's look of concern deepened, giving me an idea. If I pretended to feel a bit dizzy, maybe she would go off to get me a glass of water or something and I could take a moment to look around properly, away from her watchful eyes.

"Actually, I feel sort of dizzy all of a sudden," I said, raising my hand to my forehead in a gesture I hoped wasn't too contrived.

"Oh my," Mildred said. "You do look pale."

She went to the window and flipped the shop's *open* sign to *closed*, before locking the door.

"Why don't you come on up to my apartment? I'll get you a glass of water and you can sit down for a few minutes."

I nodded gratefully. It wasn't what I had expected to happen, but it might just be better. It would give me a chance to spot another cardigan with a button missing, or at least to ascertain whether she even had another one.

I had the vague, uneasy thought that she could be luring me up to her apartment to finish me off, but I dismissed it. Even if she was the killer, she had no reason to think I was here to investigate, and she certainly had no motive to murder me next. She was just being nice. And it wasn't like I couldn't have overpowered her, if it came to it.

"I don't suppose anyone who heard about Clayton's passing will expect the store to be open anyway, so probably no one will notice if I close up for a few minutes," Mildred added as she led me through the curtain behind the counter and to a long flight of stairs.

"It didn't occur to me that you might be closed until I was almost here, so I thought I'd check. But I must admit, I was a little surprised to see the store open," I said.

Mildred shrugged, leading me slowly up the stairs.

"The store has never closed a day, barring Christmas, for as long as I can remember—and trust me, that's a long time. I know it sounds stupid, but I guess it was my tribute to Clayton to open the store today. His attitude to any unfortunate events was always business as usual. I'm sure if he could come back, he would have told me to carry on as though nothing had happened."

"It must have come as quite a shock to you," I said. "Hearing about his death, I mean."

"It did," Mildred agreed. "And the way it happened. Just horrible. It makes you almost scared to go out at all these days, doesn't it?"

We reached the top of the stairs and Mildred opened the door and gestured for me to go in and sit down. The apartment was a studio with the bedroom and sitting room all in one. Two doors led off the room. I assumed one was the kitchen and the other was the bathroom.

"Sit down and make yourself comfortable, dear. I'll go and get you that glass of water," Mildred said.

As I took a seat, she opened the door on the right, confirming my suspicions about it leading to a kitchen.

I jumped out of my chair the second she entered the kitchen. I could hear her clanking around in there as she talked.

"Clayton wasn't the nicest man, but he didn't deserve what happened to him," she called through to me. "It really is a terrible business when you don't feel safe walking through your own town anymore, isn't it?"

I muttered my agreement as I pulled open the doors to a tall, mysterious-looking wardrobe along the wall. Clothes hung neatly on hangers. I glanced through them quickly, but there was no pink cardigan.

Mildred was still rattling around in the next room. "I used to have some aspirin around here," she was saying, presumably as she searched her kitchen cabinets. That bought me a few more precious seconds.

A quick look through a battered chest of drawers nearby confirmed there wasn't a cardigan in there either, nor was one hanging on the back of any doors or slung over any of the sparse furnishings around the room.

Sensing my time was up, I ran back to my seat, settling in place just as Mildred reappeared with a glass of water in her hand. She crossed the space and held it out to me.

"I'm afraid I couldn't find any aspirin, but maybe just the water will help," she said.

"Thank you," I said as I took it from her. "And don't worry about the pills. It isn't a headache, only dizziness."

I sipped the cool water, thinking again that despite her obvious motive, the idea of Mildred creeping around in the dead of night with a gun was a ridiculous one.

"So, what will happen to you now?" I asked. "About your apartment, I mean?"

Mildred shrugged. "I won't know for sure until Clayton's will is dealt with. My hope is that he has left the store and the apartment to someone who will be happy to see the business ticking by, making them a bit of pocket money, and not someone who will want to close it down and sell up. But who knows? At least now I have a bit of time to prepare, if I do have to move."

I took another sip of water, before standing up and holding the glass out to her. I obviously wasn't going to get anything useful here.

Anyway, as much as Betty Blackwell liked to comment on my time-keeping just because I wasn't a half hour early for everything, I didn't want to actually be late either. I knew I should be leaving.

Mildred took the glass from me and put it down on a low

coffee table that stood in the centre of two chairs and a small couch.

"Thank you so much. I feel better now and really should get going. I've taken up far too much of your time," I told her.

She waved my words away. "Nonsense. It's always nice to have a chat, isn't it? Are you sure you're feeling okay now?"

I nodded, barely concealing my impatience to be away.

"Yes, your color does seem to be returning," Mildred said.

She led me back out of her apartment and we went down to the store again.

"What was it you were hoping to find here today?" Mildred asked me as she unlocked the door and turned the sign back to *open*.

"What do you mean?" I asked.

Had she figured out that I had just wanted to poke around? Had she intentionally let me have enough time to search her clothes, thinking that would put her in the clear? She could easily have destroyed the offending cardigan altogether. For that matter, there didn't have to be any second cardigan. It could be the very one she was currently wearing, with a matching replacement button sewn on.

"Which book were you looking for?" she clarified, turning back to me.

I breathed a silent sigh of relief. Maybe she didn't know anything. She just wanted to make a sale. Since I had mentally accused her of murder, I owed her something. Buying a book was the least I could do.

"Oh, of course." I laughed. "Can you believe I almost forgot about the book? I was wondering if you had anything by Charles Dickens. I've read a lot of classics, but I never did get around to Dickens."

Mildred looked at me in horror. "Didn't get around to Dickens? My goodness, you're missing out."

She led me along the narrow aisle between two shelves and stopped in front of one, before pulling out a battered copy of Great Expectations.

"You must start with this one. It's both harrowing and beautiful, and if you enjoy it, I'd be happy to recommend some others. Dickens is one of my favorite authors."

I smiled and nodded. "That one will be perfect," I told her.

I followed her to the counter, where she wrapped the book and I got checked out. Maybe I actually would read the book. I knew the story of course, but I'd never actually read the original version. I felt like I kind of owed it to Mildred to at least try the book after she had gone out of her way to make a personal recommendation.

"Thank you," I said as I was about to leave the store. "For the book and the water. I hope everything works out for you with your apartment and the store."

"I'm sure it will. Things have a habit of working themselves out, don't they?" she replied as I left.

Out on the sidewalk, I walked back toward the truck, thinking. There had been something different about Mildred that I had been unable to place as I'd talked to her. By the time I reached the truck, it hit me what it was. She was happy. She was in her element in the bookstore, being able to help customers and make recommendations without Clayton snapping at her and breathing down her neck. It was surely a relief for her to be free of the cranky old man who had held her fate in his hands for so long.

Even so, I hadn't really found any hard evidence to link her to the crime. Even the seemingly non-existent cardigan with its missing button hadn't surfaced.

Maybe Tucker was actually right for once and the button was nothing more than a random coincidence, a button dropped by one of the hundreds of people who had been to the carnival. I really didn't like to face the idea that my instinct might have been off, but it sure seemed like that was what the evidence was saying. Everyone got lucky sometimes, I told myself, and this was just Tucker's turn to grope blindly in the dark and actually find the light switch.

12

Not too much later, I was sitting at the kettle corn stand, stirring the corn and sugar together in the large metal cauldron. I had just had a really busy couple of hours with constant lines and people wanting kettle corn. I had just about managed to keep up with the demand and had thoroughly enjoyed the busy period. It had made the thick of my time at the stand fly by and had kept my mind off both Billy and Clayton.

Of course Clayton's murder was a topic of discussion for many of the locals at the carnival, but I was just glad the incident hadn't put them off visiting today. I thought it probably helped that the crime scene tape had been taken down, no longer a constant reminder of something most people didn't want to think about.

The carnival was quieting down a bit now, though, and again my mind went back to the case. It was hard to think who would have the best motive for killing a man like Clayton. He was so dislikeable that potentially everyone who had met him might want to hurt him. I felt like it came down to working out who was the type to let an offense go, and who wasn't. But there surely had to be more to it than that. Surely no one would commit murder just because Clayton had been jerky to them. There had to be a stronger motive. Which led me straight back to square one.

Other than Mildred, who still couldn't be ruled out, who stood to gain anything by Clayton's death?

An idea flickered at the edge of my mind, a whispered conversation I vaguely remembered but couldn't place. I willed myself to dredge up the details. This could be important. It could be exactly the piece of evidence I was looking for. The truth was out there; it had to be, and this could be the key to finding it.

A child, a girl who looked around seven, came bounding happily up to my stand, accompanied by a man who was probably her dad.

"Two please," the man said as I smiled at him, awaiting his order.

After he had paid, I turned to grab the two cardboard cartons I would need and quickly filled them to bursting with the delicious snack. It was just as I was handing them over that it happened. The conversation I had been grasping at came back to me in all of its glory.

"Of course! That's it!" I shouted excitedly.

I blushed when I realized I'd spoken out loud. Both the man and his daughter were staring at me like I was crazy. I faked a laugh, trying desperately to think of something to say.

"I've had a song stuck in my head all day," I explained quickly. "And I couldn't for the life of me remember who sang it. But it just came to me."

The little girl said, "You should have asked and I could have told you. I love music and I know all the songs."

"Well, thank you. I'll remember that next time it happens." I smiled.

They seemed to buy my explanation and they made their way back into the crowd, eating their kettle corn. The girl turned back and waved to me and I returned her wave. As they left my line of sight, cutting around in the direction of the Hook A Duck stand, I allowed myself to think about what had really made me cry out in excitement.

The conversation I had remembered had happened while Suzy and I were shopping in the Baby Boutique. Charlotte Caldwell, Clayton's cousin, had been telling the family who bought the jungle gym about how she was embroiled in a legal battle with her cousin for an inheritance she felt should be hers and hers alone. It had matched with what Mildred Benson had already told me about Clayton bragging about an inheritance he would receive soon.

Charlotte definitely had a motive. If Clayton died, he was out of the picture to receive any of the inheritance and it would all be hers. And she had seemed so angry, so bitter, like someone who just might commit murder.

As soon as the conversation came back to me, I knew what I had to do, and I knew just the person to help me with it.

For the rest of my time at the kettle corn stand, I watched the hands of my watch tick around at the slowest pace they'd ever moved. I was so impatient to get over to the Baby Boutique that it almost felt as though time had stopped altogether. I told myself I had to be on the right track this time. I just hoped Suzy was free to join me at the shop.

My shift eventually ended, after what felt like a lifetime or two, and my replacement came to relieve me from the stand. I hurried back to the marquee and shed my costume quickly, not even stopping to moan to Betty about how she had tricked us all into wearing it. I would save that for another day, one where I had time to stand and make my point in the face of her denial of doing anything wrong.

As soon as I had left the carnival, crossed the parking lot, and was back in my truck, I pulled my cell phone out and called Suzy.

"Hey. Are you busy at the Posh Closet?" I asked.

"I'm always busy." She laughed. "But my shop assistant is here so if you had something in mind, I might be able to swing it. It would be nice to get out of here for a bit of fresh air, actually."

"I thought maybe we should pop back into the Baby Boutique," I told her.

"Really?" she asked, her interest clearly piqued at mention of the store. "What for?"

"Curtains," I replied, my answer already well rehearsed. "We got everything you needed for the nursery, but we didn't get any curtains. I know you probably already have some, but think about it, Suzy. Do they really match the décor in the nursery? Do they fit with what you had in mind the same way white and yellow gingham ones would?"

I crossed my fingers and waited for her response. *Please don't let her have already bought some pretty curtains that actually do match the theme of the room.*

Suzy gasped and I wasn't sure if it was a good sign or a bad one.

"Wow, Emma. You are so right. Nothing is going to look right, is it, if I just stick with the plain cream ones I was going to use? You, girl, are a genius. We have to get over there now. Meet me there in ten minutes?"

"Make it fifteen minutes and you have a deal," I said,

feeling a flood of relief that she had taken to the idea without me having to push it on her any harder. "I'm just leaving the carnival and there's a fair bit of traffic."

"Hurry up then. Get off the phone and get over here. You can't put an idea like that into my head and then leave me hanging," Suzy teased.

Sorry Brian, I thought as I hung up the phone and pulled out of the parking lot.

I felt awful, not only because I was costing Brian even more money than Suzy had already spent, but also because I had lied to my best friend. Sure, I had given her an excuse to go and do her favorite thing, but I had still lied to her. In her excitement, she hadn't considered the fact that it was out of character for me to care if her nursery curtains were cream. In fact, if she'd called me with the same story of needing white and yellow gingham curtains, I would typically have been the one trying to convince her cream was fine and went with everything.

I just didn't feel ready to tell her anything about ghosts or murder investigations, though, and if I didn't have some sort of viable cover story, or at least one that excited her enough for logic to go out the window, then she would have asked too many questions. I knew I would have ended up breaking and telling her about the ghostly visions, and in particular, Clayton Caldwell's visit.

Once upon a time, I could have considered telling Suzy the full truth and would have expected her to not only believe me, but to be supportive. But that was what I had expected from Billy too. At least for him to believe that I believed it and to accept it as a possibility. Only he hadn't. He had rejected me, and I couldn't risk losing anyone else over this. I wasn't worried about Suzy's safety. Charlotte Caldwell had made it clear in the brief moments I had spent in her store that money was her biggest motivator, and Suzy was a big spender. Charlotte would do anything to stay on Suzy's good side, including not wanting to hurt her in any way and, I hoped, maybe answering a few of my questions.

Suzy knew I had once solved the mystery of Prudence Huffler's attempted murder, of course. But she had never really pressed me for more details than I gave her, and she had no idea that most of it came down to my connection to Prudence's ghost.

No, I told myself sternly, I was right not to tell her. Not to risk telling anyone again. And it was for a good cause, so it was only a little white lie.

I felt some of the guilt leave me, but enough remained that I decided to buy a lovely cuddly white bear for the baby. Surely that would even things out.

13

Suzy and I had been shopping and chatting and laughing in the Baby Boutique for almost an hour. I had the cuddly white bear I had promised myself I would buy for the baby, now Jacob or Ava. It hadn't done as much to lessen my guilt about not telling Suzy the full truth as I had hoped it would, but I told myself once more that a murder was bigger than this and I was just doing what I had to do. It wasn't like Suzy would be hurt by the lie. It wasn't something that would affect her in any way.

Suzy had taken my advice and went for the white and yellow gingham curtains and then she had completely ignored my advice when I told her that was really all she needed. I wasn't entirely surprised by that. It was Suzy all over.

She now also had several more baby sleepers that she didn't need, half a dozen more muslin squares, even though we talked about them and admitted neither of us really knew what they were for, and a parenting book by someone I had never heard of but who Suzy insisted was a really famous blogger who everyone knew about. Everyone except me, presumably.

We were finally heading for the counter when Suzy shrieked and headed off away from it. I followed her with a sinking feeling. Last time I'd heard her make that noise, she'd spotted the rocking horse. Beautiful though it was, it was completely inappropriate for a newborn, and I feared whatever she had spotted now would be equally wrong. Then I would try and fail to talk her out of buying it.

"Aww, Emma, look at this," Suzy said. She was gently running her hand over an adorable padded white all-in-one snowsuit that had little bear ears on the hood. "Isn't it just perfect?"

I had to admit it was not only adorable, but completely age appropriate. Of course it wouldn't be winter when the baby was born, but there would always be another winter.

"It really is." I smiled. "Just make sure you get a bigger size so it will fit Jacob or Ava when next winter rolls around."

Suzy nodded and flicked through the suits until she found one in the size she was looking for. I smiled again as she held it up to show me. It really was sweet and I felt that broody feeling again.

This time, instead of a warm glow, it gave me a cold, sinking feeling. I pushed the sensation away. I hadn't told Suzy yet that Billy and I were most likely over. If I told her that, I'd have to tell her why and I hadn't come up with anything believable that didn't involve revealing the whole truth.

It was funny because Billy was the part I should have been feeling bad about. Suzy would definitely be annoyed if she found out I was keeping our probable breakup from her, yet I didn't feel guilty about it. I was barely ready to process the whole Billy thing myself, let alone discuss it with Suzy. She was likely to call him up and demand to know what he was thinking.

"Let's get out of here before I find anything else to buy," Suzy said with a grin.

"Isn't that what I've been saying for the last half an hour?" I laughed.

We made our way to the counter and Suzy handed over her things. Charlotte began to scan them.

"I was sorry to hear about the death of your cousin Clayton," I said to Charlotte.

Suzy frowned at me but I ignored her.

Charlotte shrugged. "It's fine. Stuff like that happens, right?"

"But it must have been a bit of a shock," I said, making a point of not looking at Suzy, although I could feel her gaze burning into me.

"I suppose it was, although with the way Clayton treated people, it feels like it was almost inevitable that one day he'd annoy the wrong person and end up face down in a gutter somewhere."

I nodded, hiding my shock at her answer. She had finished ringing up Suzy's things and I paused the questions while she told Suzy the total and Suzy got out her credit card and paid for the things. I handed Charlotte the bear.

"Have you heard anything from the sheriff about who might have killed Clayton?" I asked.

This time Suzy didn't just glare at me, she launched an elbow into my ribs. I side-stepped to avoid another hit.

Charlotte shook her head. "No. And quite frankly, I don't care. We were never close, and to be honest, whoever did it probably did this town a favor. My cousin was horrible to everyone, including me, and I won't be losing any sleep over what happened to him. I don't suppose you'll find anyone who will be mourning him, except perhaps Mildred Benson, his assistant at the bookstore. Although, by all accounts, it sounds like he treated her terribly too."

I tried to hide my surprise at her lack of compassion for her own kin.

Charlotte just smiled coldly as she told me how much I owed for the teddy bear. I handed over the money in cash and she rang it into the register.

"The printer is playing up. I'll handwrite you a receipt," she said.

She scrawled in a small carbon book before handing me the receipt and my change, and then Suzy and I left the store. I had nothing more to go on now than I had when I entered the boutique. Charlotte didn't seem particularly upset that Clayton was dead. In fact, I would go so far as to say she didn't care at all, but that didn't mean she was involved in the murder. Even so, I was still far from ruling her out as a suspect.

"Emma, what was all that?" Suzy demanded as we walked along Main Street.

"What was what?" I asked, although I knew exactly what she was talking about.

"That back there. Quizzing Charlotte about Clayton."

"I wasn't quizzing her. I was offering my condolences."

Suzy raised an eyebrow. "Then remind me never to call you if I need condolences."

I pretended to be offended. "Huh? I'm a great person to call for sympathy," I said.

Suzy just laughed.

We reached Posh Closet, Suzy's store, and she asked, "Are you coming in?"

I shook my head. "No, I'd better get going. I have a ton of things to do around the farm."

We hugged and said our goodbyes and I headed for my truck.

14

——————

When I told Suzy I had a ton of things to do around the farm, it wasn't an excuse, it was the truth. My back was throbbing and the muscles in my arms and legs were burning by the time I finished the last of the chores. I had almost left the wood chopping until the next morning, but I knew that would be even worse. The thought of having to leave my nice warm bed earlier than necessary to chop wood filled me with dread. And so, I had forced myself to get the job done. Now that it was, I felt glad I had made myself do it.

But my heart sank as I left the woodshed and saw a familiar, flickering figure waiting for me outside of it. The ghost of Clayton Caldwell. This was the last thing I needed right now.

"Listen up, young woman," he snapped as I approached him, "you're not making much progress with finding out who was responsible for my death, are you?"

"No, you listen up," I said back, tired of this attitude. "I'm doing the best I can and there's no need to talk to me in that manner."

He waved his hand impatiently. "Whatever," he said irritably. "I need you to investigate Sam Hanson. I've been thinking about it and I believe he's the one who killed me."

My surprise at his statement momentarily dulled my anger at his attitude.

"Sam Hanson as in Sam from Hanson's Feed and Supplies?" I asked, sure I must have heard wrong or that perhaps there was another Sam Hanson in town who I didn't know.

Clayton nodded.

I considered the idea. The young employee in the store had been visibly afraid of Sam the night I went there for chickenfeed, but I had assumed he was afraid of losing his job,not of being killed. And while Grandpa wasn't a huge fan of Sam, who he described as red-faced and bad tempered, he had never so much as hinted at the man being dangerous. The feed store owner certainly wasn't someone who would have ended up on my radar of possible murder suspects.

"Why would he do this to you?" I asked.

"To save face," Clayton replied. "I fell in his death trap of a store and he didn't want the details getting out. And he certainly didn't want to have to pay the compensation I was due."

I frowned as I remembered Mildred telling me that Clayton was suing a local business owner. She had been sure he had staged the fall and was faking his injury. I remembered seeing it for myself; Clayton's limp had kept switching sides as he walked.

It made sense that Sam would be angry with someone trying to get money out of him based on a lie and ruining his reputation in the process. But would he go so far as to kill? It did sound like he had more to lose with Clayton alive than he did with him dead, but surely Clayton wouldn't have actually won the lawsuit, and Sam would have been vindicated without having to murder anyone.

I was fast running out of options, though, and Sam at least had a motive, even if it was a bit of a flimsy one. I nodded my head.

"I'll look into him," I promised.

"Good," Clayton said. "Because I'm getting awfully tired of waiting for justice."

With that, he vanished and I was once more alone in the yard. I walked the rest of the way back to the house, lost in thought.

I walked into the kitchen to find Grandma ready to serve dinner.

"Do me a favor, Emma. Pop out to the shed and tell your grandpa dinner is ready," she said.

I hurried back out to the shed with Snowball at my feet and relayed the message to Grandpa. He was ready to finish up for the day, so we walked back up to the house together. Dinner was plated and ready for us to tuck in. I sat down and began to hungrily work on the beef casserole Grandma had made. It was packed full of homemade dumplings that were just the right balance of crispiness and melt-in-your-mouth deliciousness.

An idea of how I could find out more about Sam came to me as we ate, and I turned to Grandpa.

"Did you ever manage to find out the expected delivery date of the things you ordered from Hanson's?" I asked.

Grandpa nodded. "Yes. They're due any day now and Sam said he'll call me the moment they arrive."

"Let me know when they come in, and I'll go and collect them for you," I said.

Grandpa shook his head. "Nah," he said. "I'll make sure and be the one to deal with Sam."

That set off an alarm bell in my brain. My question had been to test the waters. If Grandpa had agreed, it would've meant he didn't think Sam was dangerous, as he would never knowingly send me into danger. I had been to the store a few times, but always with Grandpa, except the one time I collected Grandma's chickenfeed, and I wasn't sure Grandpa even knew in advance I was going to do that.

I had to know more, but I didn't want to raise Grandpa's suspicions. If he knew I was involved in another murder investigation, it would only worry him and I would rather not have him worried on my behalf.

I gave a little laugh. "You make it sound like you don't trust him very much," I said.

Grandpa frowned and shook his head. "He's not the nicest fellow, but I wouldn't say he's untrustworthy. I just want to make sure everything in the order is right, that's all."

I nodded and went back to eating my dinner. So Grandpa evidently didn't think Sam was dangerous. That didn't necessarily rule him out as a suspect for Clayton's murder, of course.

I wanted to ask more. Like if Grandpa knew about the lawsuit and how Sam had reacted to it. But I knew anything else would raise my grandpa's suspicions so I pushed the idea to one side. I would find another way to investigate Sam, one that left my grandpa out of it.

"How was your day, Grandma?" I asked.

"Fine, thank you," she said. "I went into town earlier and got a few bits. I ran into Vera Harrison. Her granddaughter is expecting and due any day now. They were told long ago that she would never have children, so everyone's really excited about the *miracle baby*, as they're calling it."

"Oh, that's lovely," I said. "That baby is going to be spoilt rotten."

Grandma nodded and laughed. "That's for sure."

After we finished eating dinner and clearing the dishes away, I announced I was going up to my room. I was tired and an early night would do me a world of good. I kissed my grandparents goodnight and went to my room, Snowball running on up ahead of me.

I changed into my nightclothes and got into bed. Snowball was already curled up at the bottom of the blankets. I lay back for a moment thinking of Suzy and Vera Harrison's granddaughter. I wondered vaguely whether either of them were truly prepared for motherhood and how it would change them, and I felt the broodiness again. I knew it would pass, or at least I hoped it would. I just wanted it to be sooner rather than later.

As I thought of babies, my thoughts inevitably turned back to Billy. I was conscious of the fact I hadn't heard from him since our disastrous dinner and I felt both confused and annoyed. Billy had acted strangely, that was for sure, but he didn't actually come out and say we were over. I felt like I was floating in limbo.

I reached for my cell phone and opened up a new text message. I had no idea what to say. I wasn't the one who needed to apologise. He was. I put the phone back down on my nightstand, the message unwritten.

After the way Billy had reacted to my confession about being an amateur sleuth on behalf of the town's ghosts, I felt as though the ball was very firmly in his court. I would just have to accept that if I didn't hear from him, then it was over.

I switched off my lamp, sure sleep would claim me in seconds, but it seemed that I was now wide awake, thoughts of Billy swirling through my mind. I sighed loudly and pushed the emotions away. I was only torturing myself.

As I shoved Billy's image from my mind, it was replaced with the image of Clayton Caldwell. I began to think again whether or not Sam Hanson could possibly be responsible for the murder. An idea started to form in my mind of how I could work out if he was at least a contender.

With the plan in place, my eyelids finally began to get heavy. I fell into a deep sleep, knowing what I would do tomorrow.

15

The next morning, I pulled up in the parking lot outside of Hanson's Feed and Supplies and hopped down from the truck's cab. I hurried into the store and grinned to myself when I saw the young man from the other night was at the counter again. Finally, a stroke of luck.

I grabbed a bag of cat food as an excuse for being here. Our barn cat, Pudding, who I had brought back from my last visit to New York, was low on food anyway. Next I made my way up to the counter, where the familiar employee smiled when he saw me.

While I was paying for the cat food, I remembered to ask him if he would be able to check on the progress of my grandpa's order. He nodded and turned to his computer screen. As he clicked away at a few buttons, I knew I had to find a way to start questioning him. I had the perfect lead-in.

"I hope I didn't get you in any trouble the other night when I was here so late," I said.

The young man shook his curly head. "No, it was fine.

Mr Hanson arrived just after you left and no one else had come in."

"You sounded almost scared of him," I said.

"Not of him, as such. I just need this job," he said.

I smiled. "Then I guess you're pretty relieved that the whole Clayton Caldwell lawsuit has gone away," I said. "You know, in case Sam got taken to the cleaners and had to let the store go."

"From what I've heard, that was never going to happen. Sam's lawyer apparently had proof that Clayton was faking the injury," he said quietly.

"Sam must have been angry, though, right? I mean, to have the whole town talking about him as though he'd caused an injury to a customer couldn't be good for business, could it?"

The young man's face changed, the color draining out of his round cheeks. He wouldn't even look at me.

Suddenly, I felt a strong hand clamp down on my shoulder. Startled, I whirled around.

"That's enough gossip from you, lady," the man who had grabbed me said, lowering his hand to his side but still glaring down into my face.

He towered over me, a broad-shouldered, square-jawed man in rough clothes. He had a muscular build, despite the flecks of gray in his hair, and wore an intimidating expression across his reddish face.

"What?" I asked, more surprised than angry. My shoulder smarted where his thick hand had briefly rested.

"I want you to leave my store," he demanded, angrier now. "How dare you come in here gossiping about my business and questioning my employees about that fake lawsuit? As if it wasn't enough that Clayton was trying to ruin my reputation when he was alive, now it seems he's still doing it from beyond the grave."

I started to back away when I realized this must be Sam Hanson. And he had caught me talking about him.

Even as I backed toward the doors, he followed me, not done yet.

"While you seem so intent on putting your nose into someone else's business, then why don't you at least spread the truth around? The day before Clayton was killed, I ran into him in the parking lot of the carnival. I told him about the evidence my lawyer had, a video of him walking perfectly normally down a public street, with no sign of his fake limp. Clayton argued for a while, naturally, but he finally agreed to drop the lawsuit. And then someone killed him, and now no one will ever believe he made all that up about my store. Spread that around, why don't you?"

"I ... I will," I said.

I had stopped backing away now as curiosity got the better of me. From what Sam said, he must have been the man I had seen Clayton arguing with in the parking lot of the carnival while I was up on the Ferris wheel. And if Sam was telling the truth about Clayton agreeing to drop the lawsuit, then he had no motive for the murder. But he could well be lying, and it was still possible that he had somehow lured Clayton back to the carnival that night and killed him.

I opened my mouth to ask Sam a question, but he cut me off.

"You have quite enough gossip about me now, thank you. So please leave this store and don't come back," he snapped, yanking one of the front double-doors open and waiting for me to leave.

Unable to think of anything more to say, I hurried past

him, my cheeks burning with shame at having been caught in my snooping. Some sleuth I was.

My efforts had turned up information—the fact that Sam Hanson was an unpleasant man with a bad temper—but once again, I had no definite proof of wrong-doing.

I had to come up with a plan to find the truth. And I had to do it fast. Every day that went by would give the murderer, whoever they really were, a chance to destroy any evidence of guilt.

16

After my visit to Hanson's, my day's work at the carnival was long and uneventful, but at least it gave me time to think about my investigation. I was still thinking on the drive home that evening and all the way through dinner with my grandparents, which we ate mostly in silence. My mind was too occupied for small talk and Grandma and Grandpa seemed too tired from their chores around the farm to engage in idle chatter.

Later, as I lay upstairs in bed, waiting to hear the sounds of my grandparents turning in for the night, I considered my next move. I knew what I had to do to help me work out who had murdered Clayton, and at the time that I had gotten the idea (while I was working on the kettle corn stand earlier – that alone time really seemed to get my brain ticking) I had thought it was the obvious solution. Now that it was time to really put my plan into action, though, I wasn't so sure it was a good idea after all. But it was the only one I had. The only thing I could think of that might be able to help me out here. I kept coming up with a blank everywhere else I turned.

I kept my ears trained on the small sounds filtering up from downstairs, waiting until all grew quiet, indicating my grandparents had finally turned in. Then I slipped back out of my bed. I was already fully dressed because I'd kept my clothes on under the covers. I'd half expected my grandma to come up to say goodnight, so I'd been careful to keep under the blanket until I was satisfied she was asleep in her room. Luckily, she and Grandpa had stuck to their usual nightly routine.

My plan was to break into Clayton Caldwell's house and try to find some clue there as to who his murderer could possibly be. I could justify breaking and entering, in my own mind. After all, it was Clayton's house I'd be breaking into, and Clayton's ghost had come and asked me to solve this crime. It was almost an invite. That was a good enough reason for me. And, of course I had no intention of stealing or damaging anything. But that would hardly wash if I got caught, would it?

Even Tucker wouldn't believe that I had implied permission from Clayton's ghost to enter his house as I was trying to solve his murder. The sheriff might believe my ultimate intentions were good, but I could never tell him the full truth about Clayton's ghost demanding my help. It would look like I just had some sort of hero complex that had gotten completely out of hand.

My heart was in my throat as I crept downstairs, carefully avoiding the creakiest attic steps. It wasn't really being caught by my grandparents that worried me. There were worse things that could go wrong once I left the house. I swallowed hard, trying to get rid of the nerves that filled me, making my mouth dry and my heart beat too fast against my ribs. I felt a little nauseous, too. I reminded myself this was my only option – I couldn't see any other way of finding the information I needed.

I took a deep breath as I crossed the darkened living room. Everything would be fine. All I had to do was get in, find what I needed, and get back out of Clayton's house. All without getting caught, of course. That would be the hardest part. It seemed like literally everyone in town was nosey, and the slightest bit of noise from a dead man's house would have the vultures circling in minutes. I couldn't let the idea of being caught stop me, though. I would just have to be extra careful.

I slipped out the front door of the farmhouse, careful to close it quietly behind me. It wouldn't do to have my plan thwarted already because my grandparents heard me sneaking out. I had a plan in place to cover me if that happened. I was just going to say I had forgotten my cell phone in the truck earlier. There was no reason they wouldn't believe me.

I sneaked across to the battered old vehicle and got in. Inserting the key, I cringed at the loud roar as the engine came to life. Again, I had a plan in place for this part. If I was caught by either of my grandparents, I would say I couldn't sleep and I was just annoying myself tossing and turning so I had decided to go for a drive around. It sounded a bit far-fetched, but no one would guess that I was actually going to break into someone's house.

I watched the farmhouse, hardly daring to breath, but no lights came on and the front door didn't burst open. So far so good, I thought to myself as I pulled away. Maybe luck was on my side for once.

Earlier, I had asked around among the carnival volunteers and learned where Clayton Caldwell had lived. Importantly for my plan, I discovered he had lived alone. I had even driven by his place on my way home this evening to be sure I had the right address, although I had decided to wait for nightfall before risking trespassing on the property.

The roads were deserted now, as I drove through town towards Clayton's house. It was so quiet I felt like a criminal already and I hadn't even done anything wrong yet. It was one of those times I missed the hustle and bustle of the city. It was much easier to blend in on a night when the place was buzzing with people, no matter how late the hour might be.

I parked the truck a couple of blocks away from Clayton's place and grabbed my bag of burglary supplies off the seat. Not that I really knew what to bring to a break-in, but certain items, such as a flashlight and prying tools, seemed like a given. I was nervous again as I jumped out of the vehicle and made my way forward, staying close against nearby buildings, hoping to hide in the shadows. Clayton's house was in a run-down neighbourhood, surrounded at a distance by similar, decaying homes that had seen better days. I was grateful that the houses were at least spaced far apart, far enough that, with any luck, my arrival would escape the notice of any neighbours who might happen to be up and glancing out their windows at this hour.

The black jeans and hoodie I had worn would help me to meld into the shadows, too. The hood was drawn and the only visible skin was my face. Black gloves kept my hands hidden.

You're fine, I told myself. Don't panic and just keep moving. You've got this. I wasn't overly convinced by my own assurances, but I hadn't come all this way to back out now.

I finally reached Clayton's place, and strangely, now that I was at the point in my plan where I was actually breaking the law, I felt suddenly calm. I wanted to take advantage of the calmness that washed over me, so I quickly made my way through the garden and around to the back of the house. I opened up my bag and pulled out a crowbar, which I used to break the lock on the back door. I was relying heavily on the fact that ours was one of those towns where locks were more something people had out of habit, rather than any real need for security. There would be no additional measures. No alarm and certainly no CCTV. It made my job tonight a bit easier.

I stepped into Clayton's kitchen and pushed the door shut behind me. Pausing, I waited to see if any nosy neighbour had spotted me and would come to investigate. After a few moments, I told myself if anyone was coming they'd be here by now and if they had called the police, it was too late for me to do anything about it.

As satisfied with my progress as I could be, I pulled a penlight out of my bag. I wanted to see where I was going but didn't want to light the place up like a lighthouse in a storm. I made my way through the kitchen, looking for an office of some kind. I poked my head into the first door. A living room. I figured it was unlikely there would be anything useful in there, so I kept going. The next space was a rather bare dining room, containing a table and chairs and nothing else. Finally, I stumbled across what I was looking for. It wasn't exactly an office. It was more of a library, with books lining one wall and a reading nook set up in a corner. But in the opposite corner a filing cabinet and a big pinewood desk stood. I figured if there was anything in here that could help me, it would be in one of those two places.

I moved over to the area, deciding to tackle the file cabinet first. The top drawer contained financial accounts for the bookstore, as well as Mildred Benson's rental agreement. I had a quick glance over them. Nothing jumped out at me as particularly wrong, but I was no financial wizard or contract law expert, and I really had very little idea of what I was looking at. Nothing set alarm bells ringing inside me, though, so I thought it would be best to move on. I could always take another look in the drawer if I didn't find anything more interesting first. The next drawer was empty, and the bottom one contained a bunch of unused stationary and accounting pads. That left the desk.

I opened the top desk drawer and rummaged around. It contained a lot of receipts and a few invoices. Beneath the pile of invoices was an envelope with Clayton's name scrawled on it in ink. That caught my attention. A hand-written note would surely be more likely to have something useful in it than a standard invoice from a book wholesaler. I didn't like to rule anyone out prematurely, but even I had to admit it was unlikely some book dealer from Ohio would come all the way to Hillbilly Hollow, Missouri, to kill Clayton Caldwell.

I picked up the envelope, my loose-fitting gloves making my hands clumsy. I debated taking them off, but I knew that was a bad idea. If Tucker ever decided to fingerprint-check anything in the house, I didn't want my prints all over Clayton's belongings. The gloves stayed on.

I opened the envelope where Clayton had tucked the ragged flap back inside it, and pulled out a single sheet of paper. On it was written the following:

It's time we settled our differences once and for all in a neutral location. Meet me at the parking lot in front of the carnival at midnight. We have a lot to discuss and it's in both our interests to deal with this quickly.

· · ·

THE LETTER WASN'T SIGNED, and I could see why. At first glance, it read like a reasonable request for two adults to have a civil discussion. But in light of Clayton's fate, there was a definite feeling of threat to the letter. And the suggestion of meeting in an empty parking lot at midnight did little to make the note sound any friendlier.

I debated returning it to where I had found it, but a little voice in the back of my mind told me that was a bad idea. There was a good chance whoever had sent the message would be itching to destroy it, and they might well just be waiting for the dust to settle and the investigation to tail off before they came here for that purpose.

I dug into my bag again and removed a clear plastic baggy. It would hopefully keep any existing forensic evidence like fingerprints or skin cells in place and usable. But of course I couldn't take the note to the police yet. I would've had to explain how I got it and that would lead to an extremely unpleasant conversation. All the note proved right now was that Clayton's murder may have been planned – something I thought everyone in town, except Tucker, already believed. Maybe even Tucker had by now come to suspect as much.

Finding nothing else of interest during a quick search of the other rooms, I went through the kitchen again and slipped back out of Clayton's house, closing the back door behind me. I hurried to my truck and was relieved to be out of there and away from danger, as I started the engine and drove back to the farm.

Back home, I managed to sneak into the farmhouse and get to my attic room without waking my grandparents. As far as I knew, I hadn't been spotted by anyone tonight.

As I entered my room, Snowball looked up from where

she was curled at the foot of my bed and gave an angry bleat, probably unhappy that I had left her behind.

"Sorry, girl," I muttered absently. "Burglary is no business for goats."

I took the baggie containing the note from my bag and reread the message without taking it out of the plastic. I wondered vaguely why Clayton's ghost hadn't mentioned the note to me. If he had, it would have saved a lot of sneaking around. Maybe he was embarrassed by how easily he had been lured to his death. In his defence, though, he might have expected trouble but he probably hadn't expected to be shot and killed. It made sense that he had gone to the meeting, thinking whatever issue he had with the sender would finally be resolved.

And the best explanation I could think of for why he had kept it a secret from me was that maybe it wasn't so much a secret as something he didn't think was important. Anyway, maybe even he didn't know who the anonymous sender was. Or maybe he did. It could be that the sender had been Sam Hanson, in which case, the letter would seem irrelevant to Clayton, as he had already told me in no uncertain terms to look into Sam. It would make sense that Clayton would go to meet Sam if he thought the letter was from him.

In fact, the more I thought about it, the more I convinced myself Sam Hanson really was behind this. From his brusque manner with me in the shop to his obvious issues with Clayton, he fit the bill for the killer. But I still couldn't prove any of it.

Of course, there was still Clayton's cousin Charlotte to think about. There certainly seemed to be a lot of bad feeling between them and the inheritance dispute would give them motive for a quarrel and a secret meeting to try and resolve it.

I wasn't ready to discount Mildred either, for all her sweet old lady persona. She had more reason than anyone to want Clayton dead, and not just because he was a bad boss. He could have taken away her job and her home in an instant if any of his money-making schemes were ever successful enough to allow him to sell the bookshop. Mildred was another potential sender of the note.

My head was aching, partly from the constant swirl of thoughts and partly from the lack of sleep caused by my creeping around through the night. I decided to worry about this tomorrow. For now, I desperately needed to get some sleep. My eyes felt gritty and sore. I climbed into bed still fully clothed, lacking the energy to get undressed.

Glancing at the clock, I could have cried when I saw the time. I had around half an hour before I would have to get up and sort out the wood burner. Oh well, I told myself. If this note somehow put me on the right track to solving the case, it was worth a sleepless night.

17

A s I walked into the marquee at the carnival the next day, my mind was still swimming with thoughts of Clayton and the note I had found. It didn't help that I was so tired. I had already had three large black coffees and now I was worried about whether or not my bladder would cooperate through my full shift at the kettle corn stand, as well as whether I could stay awake.

Betty Blackwell was once more seated behind her makeshift desk as I entered the marquee. She not-very-subtly checked the time as I approached her desk and the screened off area behind it. I wasn't late, even though today of all days I felt like it would have been perfectly excusable if I was. My tiredness, the confusion and frustration surrounding Clayton's murder, and my crushing sadness that Billy still hadn't been in touch, all came together as Betty looked at her watch and then at me.

Suddenly I knew I couldn't face another day in that awful costume, and nothing Betty could say would be able to change my mind about that.

"I won't be wearing anything except the clothes I'm

standing in today, Betty. If you feel that's an unacceptable way for me to represent the historical society in public, then I'd be perfectly happy to take over here signing people in and out and letting you run the stall."

Betty flushed red and opened and closed her mouth a couple of times. But she must have seen by the set of my mouth that I was serious, because after a moment, she nodded.

"Okay, fine. You can wear your own clothes if that will make you more comfortable," she said.

I nodded at her and walked back towards the entrance to the marquee. My purse was stashed underneath my seat in the truck and my cell phone was in my pocket.

"Emma, wait," Betty's voice rang out from behind me.

Frustration welled up inside me, but I did my best not to sigh. As much as I was enjoying the carnival and doing my bit for the historical society, if Betty became too much to bear today, I knew I would walk away from it all.

I paused and waited for her to catch up. She took me by my elbow and led me back towards the screen.

"I'm serious, Betty. I'm not wearing it. Now, I should go. I'm going to be late to take over the stall," I said as calmly as I could manage.

"Andrew can wait five minutes for you to replace him at the stall. It won't kill him to make a little more kettle corn," Betty said.

I doubted my fellow volunteer, Andrew, would agree with that but I bit my tongue.

She got me back behind the screen and stood looking at me.

"Well?" she demanded.

"Well what?" I asked, genuinely confused.

"What's wrong, Emma?"

"Nothing is wrong," I started, but Betty cut me off.

"Look, I know you and Beth worked out on the first day that the costume was my idea, and yet you wore it anyway. And I know sometimes I can be rather overbearing, and yet you've never been short with me like this before. So, out with it. What's the matter?"

She sounded genuinely sympathetic and she was peering at me with a frown of concern. I suddenly felt awful that I had taken my stress out on her. Not awful enough to relent and wear the costume, but awful enough that I knew I had to apologise.

"I'm sorry, Betty." I sighed. "I'm really not in the mood to wear a costume, but I shouldn't have snapped at you like that."

Betty waved away my apology. "I don't care about that. I care about what's wrong with you. I've rarely seen you without a smile on your face, since you joined us. It's not your grandparents, is it?"

"Oh no, they're both fine, I promise you. I just didn't sleep much last night, and ..."

I trailed off, horrified that I had almost announced my thoughts about the note I'd found in Clayton's house.

"And?" Betty prompted.

I had to tell her something.

"And I'm a bit stressed out about some freelance design work I'm doing for a client online," I said.

"Are you sure that's all it is?" she asked.

I nodded, although I felt a little bad about the lie.

"Do you need to take a day off? I can cover for you or ask one of the other volunteers to switch with you," Betty said.

I shook my head. "No, honestly, that's the last thing I need. It will do me good to get some fresh air and take in the carnival atmosphere," I said.

That much at least was completely true.

"Well, you just let me know if you change your mind, okay?" she said.

I nodded again. "I will. Thanks Betty."

I had been surprised by her concern, and I promised myself I'd go easier on her next time she was short with me. I started to walk away when she called after me again.

"Don't worry. He'll call."

I turned around, my jaw open, and Betty smiled.

"That handsome doctor of yours, I mean. Whatever lover's tiff you two have had, he's not stupid. He won't let a catch like you get away." She smiled.

I found myself shocked by her, once more. I had no idea most people had even noticed Billy and I were a thing, let alone that my heartbreak was written all over my face.

"I mean, it's not like there's a lot of choice around here, is it?" Betty added.

I genuinely smiled for what felt like the first time that day. It had been nice to see the softer side of Betty, but it was also nice to have the old Betty back. I surprised both of us by crossing the distance and embracing her. She hugged me stiffly in return and then jumped back, smoothing her hair.

"That's the first time I've smiled all day. Thank you," I said.

"Well, we're a team here, Emma, and we do what we can for each other," she said.

She was blushing, and although she acted like she was embarrassed by my hug, I thought she was secretly quite pleased.

"Off you go now, dear. Andrew will be wondering where you've got to."

I left the marquee before there could be any more surprises and hurried to the stand.

"I'm sorry I'm late," I said to Andrew.

He looked at me and smiled. "Wow. You must have been really late for Betty to let you get away with not wearing the costume."

"Yes, I was," I agreed.

That was one way I could repay Betty's small kindness. If I told anyone I had refused to wear the outfit and worked at the stand anyway, they would all refuse to wear it again, too. This way, Betty could hold the others to it, and for the couple more shifts I had before the carnival was over, I would wear it also. I kind of owed her that much now.

Andrew left the stall and I rearranged a few things, getting it back to the set up I liked. I sat down on my stool and settled in for a few mindless hours of stirring popcorn and sugar together.

A family walked up to the stall and asked for four portions of kettle corn. The two small children were excitable, their faces shining and their giggles infectious.

As I talked to them, I felt eyes boring into my back. I turned around but no one was there. I told myself I was being paranoid, that someone was probably just glancing over at the stall as they passed by.

But no matter how much I tried to reassure myself over the next three hours, I constantly felt like I was being watched, although I never actually saw anyone spying on me. I decided I would have an early night tonight and maybe wake up in the morning without these silly imaginings. I couldn't cope with another day like this. Being over-tired really didn't work well for me and I wondered how other people did it. People who worked nights and things like that. I was definitely no night owl.

A short line formed at the stall, and as I quickly put the kettle corn into the cardboard containers and took the money for each portion, the time whizzed by. I no longer had a spare second to think about who would want to watch me or why.

When the rush finally dissipated, I picked up another bag of popcorn and emptied it into the cauldron. I reached for a bag of sugar and as I lifted it, I saw a long white envelope propped between two bags of sugar. It bore only one word. *Emma.*

Distracted, I hurried to pour the sugar into the cauldron. Then I snatched up the envelope and pocketed it with one hand while I stirred the mixture with the other, telling myself I would read whatever was inside after my shift.

I couldn't wait, though. It felt as though the envelope was burning a hole in my pocket. As soon as the kettle corn was stirred enough for me to be able to pause for a moment without it congealing, I pulled the envelope back out. I turned it over in my hands, looking for anything other than my name written anywhere on it. There was nothing else.

My heart raced the longer I studied my name scribbled across the front. I realized I knew that handwriting. It was the same handwriting as the note I had found in Clayton Caldwell's house. I tore the envelope open in one quick rip before I could change my mind. When I pulled out a single sheet of paper, it was the same plain white paper that Clayton's note had been written on.

STOP SNOOPING *into things that are none of your business, or I will stop you.*

THAT WAS IT. Just one chilling sentence that sent a shiver down my spine. If I had any sense at all, I would heed the warning and give up my work on the case. Instead, the order riled me up, and made me all the more determined to find the killer. How dare they threaten me in this way?

I read the note again and as I did, something clicked in my mind. The note I had found in Clayton's house wasn't the only place where I had seen that handwriting before. I was almost certain of it.

And if I was right, I now had enough evidence to take to Tucker. I just had to get confirmation first that I was remembering correctly.

18

As Beth arrived at the kettle corn stand to take over for me, I hid my mouth with my hand so she couldn't see me smiling at her in the costume. She looked kind of ridiculous, but also kind of adorable.

"So apparently the trick is to arrive so late you don't have time to put it on, huh?" Beth said, spotting my smile immediately and shaking her head in mock exasperation.

I nodded. "Yeah. That's the trick," I agreed.

Andrew had obviously mentioned my excuse about being late to Betty, who had played along as I figured she would. It seemed it had all worked out as I had hoped.

"Thing is, though, Emma, as much as I hate wearing this stupid thing, I'd rather wear it than have Betty go off on me about being late. For an old woman, she's darned scary, isn't she? How bad was it when you showed up late? Did you feel like crying?"

"Bad," I said with a laugh. "Not quite bad enough that I felt like crying, but bad enough that I'll be making sure I'm early for anything she's in charge of from now to eternity."

I didn't feel guilty about that lie. Betty would be pleased

that I was upholding her reputation as the timekeeper, rather than upset that I was making her out to be the bad guy. Even though I'd seen a different side to her, I still knew she relished her tough role, and who was I to take that away from her? Especially with Beth, who, like me, had once seen the softer side of Betty. I suspected her unwillingness to turn up late and not wear the costume was more to do with that than with her being genuinely afraid of Betty's wrath.

Beth took her place at the kettle corn stand and smiled as she looked out across the carnival.

"I love working this shift. Everything's so pretty with all the lights lit up, isn't it?"

I had to agree with her. It really was a sight to behold, and the darkness and the cold did nothing to dilute the party atmosphere.

"Yeah, it's beautiful alright. Well, I'd best get going," I said. "Have fun."

"I will," Beth replied. "You too."

"Always," I shouted back as I walked away.

I didn't think what I was about to do would be exactly fun, but it would take a whole lot of stress away from me. The excitement of working out who had written the note had kept me going for the last hour or so of my shift, and now, knowing what I was about to do, adrenaline coursed through my body, keeping me alert and making me forget how tired I had been earlier.

I hurried towards the parking lot and my truck. I was pleased I'd left my purse in the vehicle today. It meant I didn't have to waste time going back to the marquee and possibly getting caught up in a conversation with Betty or one of the other volunteers. I needed to move fast if I was to catch what I needed to see tonight. And I knew I had to see it tonight. I didn't think my nerves could stand another night on edge, wondering if I had gotten it wrong.

I clambered into the truck, started the engine, and pulled away, not bothering to wait for the cab to heat up, as I normally did. I headed towards the shops of Main Street, but as I approached my usual parking area, I changed my mind and kept driving. I headed around the back of the stores instead and drove past the big parking lot. It was almost empty, since the shops were closing for the night. I parked a block behind the big parking lot and jumped down from the truck, cutting through the almost deserted area.

I ducked down a short alley and hurried past a couple shops, until I reached the one I wanted. The Baby Boutique. I pushed the door but it was locked, Charlotte already having closed it for the evening. But it was okay. The shutters were still open and the dim light left on inside was enough that I could see what I had come for.

Suddenly, I thought I spotted movement in the store. Heart pounding, I crouched down out of sight. But when nothing else stirred, I told myself I was being paranoid again. Even if Charlotte was in there, it wasn't like it was a crime to look into a store window. That was kind of the point of putting displays in them. If she came out and questioned me, I could bluff that I was looking for something for Suzy. I straightened back up and pressed my face to the window in the door, peering into the gloomy store.

There it was. A handwritten sign advertising various sale products. It confirmed the truth. The handwriting matched the note I had found in Clayton's house, the other note that was still in my pocket, and the handwritten receipt Charlotte had given me for the bear for Suzy's baby. That was how I had worked out who had left me the note. I had remembered seeing the writing before, and it just came to me all of a sudden that I had first seen it on the receipt. Of course I had given the bag containing the receipt to Suzy, along with the bear, which was why I had to come back here and find a further example of Charlotte's handwriting. I'd had to confirm to myself that I wasn't misremembering.

Now that I was satisfied my mind hadn't played a trick on me, it wasn't only myself I needed to confirm the truth for. I pulled my cell phone out of my pocket and opened the camera app. I zoomed in and snapped off a couple of photographs of the sign to show to Tucker. For someone so lost in his job, it often took a while to convince the sheriff of an idea. My having a photo of the sign that showed the handwriting matched that on the notes would save me a lot of time and convincing. Tucker would have to take me seriously about this.

I quickly looked through the pictures I had taken, making sure the handwriting was clear on at least one of them. It was. Satisfied, I put my phone back in my pocket and hurried away back the way I had come. I would drive straight over to the police station and find Tucker right now.

As I walked down the alley connecting the main street with the parking lot behind it, I heard footsteps behind me. I quickened my pace slightly, telling myself to calm down. It would be a worker from one of the stores going to his or her car, that was all.

When I entered the parking lot, the footsteps kept pace with me. The hairs on the back of my neck stood up. I was being followed. I spun around and found myself face to face with a sneering Charlotte Caldwell.

I felt a chill run down my spine as I glanced to my left and right and saw we were completely alone. It wasn't lost on me that I was in a deserted parking lot with someone who had recently committed a murder in a very similar location. It definitely wasn't the best situation I had ever found myself in.

I tried not to panic but that was easier said than done.

I didn't have anything on me that I could use as a weapon. There was at least a fifty-fifty chance that Charlotte was carrying a gun, and I knew from the fact she had shot Clayton in the back that she wasn't afraid to use it. And he was a family member; there was no way she was going to spare me if she didn't spare him. The only thing I could think to do was to try and keep her distracted long enough for someone else to appear in the parking lot. Maybe then I could use that moment to make my getaway. I was almost sure she wouldn't want to gun me down in front of a witness and then have to deal with them as well.

I tried to think what to say to start a conversation with her, but my mind came up blank. *Why did you kill your cousin?* That question seemed a bit too forward to ask aloud. Anyway, there was still the smallest chance she didn't know I knew what she had done. But I didn't place too much hope in that chance. If she didn't know, why else would she have risked leaving me the note?

Charlotte actually came to my rescue, starting the conversation for me.

"You just couldn't do it, could you? Couldn't mind your own business. You always were nosey. Always poking your oversized beak into things that didn't concern you, even when we were in high-school."

My hand automatically went to my nose, self-consciously touching it to investigate whether it really was oversized.

Charlotte laughed nastily. "Little goody two shoes Emma with her hero complex, running to the teacher about other people," she said. "I should have known you'd have to get involved in this. You know the good thing about this town, though? The sheriff's an idiot. I'd have gotten away with this if you hadn't been poking around. And do you want to know something else? I'm still going to. You were warned, and what was the first thing you did? Ignored the warning. That was a mistake, Emma. One that will cost you your life."

I knew I had to do or say something to keep Charlotte from carrying out her threat.

"I don't understand," I said. "Why did you do it, Charlotte?"

"Why did I kill Clayton? Have you met the man?"

Well, yes, I got that he was abrasive, but she wasn't exactly sunshine and roses herself. There had to be more to it than his attitude. It had to be about the money.

As if reading my mind, Charlotte said, "You're the amateur sleuth, you figure it out."

She smiled, a predatory smile that sent a shiver up my spine. But if she was going to kill me anyway, I might as well at least find out the truth. So rather than trying to find the right words to calm her down, instead, I settled on telling her my honest thoughts.

"I'd hazard a guess it was to do with the fact you didn't want to share the family inheritance with your cousin. But I don't get it. You both had successful businesses and neither of you really needed the money that badly. Why kill for it?"

"Clayton was always jealous that my store was more profitable than his. I told him loads of times why that was, but in typical Clayton fashion, he wouldn't listen. I sell something customers want and are willing to spend money on. It's funny, even people who say they are struggling financially find the extra money when it comes to buying stuff for their little poop machines. I mean, you know yourself from the way your friend Suzy went on in the store, don't you?

Who orders a rocking horse for a newborn? Expectant first time mothers who want it all, that's who. I told Clayton the book trade is a dying business, but he wouldn't listen to me. So yeah, my store was more successful than his ever was."

"I still don't get it. That sounds more like a motive for him to kill you," I replied.

I knew I was on shaky ground, but her explanation didn't make any sense.

Charlotte rolled her eyes and went on. "My uncle's will stated that Clayton and I, as the only remaining family members, should share his assets fifty-fifty. But I realized if I sold the Baby Boutique, coupled with the amount of the full inheritance, I could retire and live very comfortably for the next forty or fifty years. The only problem with my plan was that Clayton stood in the way. Luckily, I learned at an early age that the only way to survive in this life is to see what you want and take it. And that's what I do. And now my problem is you. You're standing in the way of my freedom. And I can't have that, can I?"

I knew the time was coming for her to take action, and the parking lot was still deserted. I had to make my own move first. Now that I'd had time to consider it, it seemed unlikely that Charlotte still had the gun with her that she had used to kill Clayton. She was no fool and would have dumped the murder weapon by now, just in case the police came around asking questions. So, it was more likely that she had a knife or other weapon she meant to silence me with.

That left me with two choices. I could try to overpower her right here. Or I could outrun her and head straight for the police station. I didn't think I would be able to beat her in a fight for my life. Although slim, she was muscular and looked like she'd be able to hold her own. More importantly, she wouldn't have challenged my life like this unless she had some extra advantage up her sleeve, most likely a sharp instrument. Then too, even after what she'd done, I didn't particularly want to hurt her. My reluctance to seriously injure her would put me at a distinct disadvantage, because she definitely wanted to hurt me.

No, I thought to myself, my best bet was trying to escape her. I was fast on my feet, and since I'd come back to town and begun helping out around the farm again, I had lost the extra couple of pounds I'd carried in the city. I was definitely the fittest I had ever been and was pretty sure I could outrun her without breaking a sweat.

Of course, that'd give Charlotte a chance to skip town if she chose to do the sensible thing, rather than chasing after me. But as long as I reported what I knew to the police, it wasn't my problem to hunt her down. And if she fled town, she'd actually have a better chance of being caught because she would leave Tucker's jurisdiction and hopefully land someplace with a sheriff who didn't struggle to find his own feet in the dark. Yes, this plan could actually work, both to save me life and get Charlotte taken into custody.

I had made my decision. I turned and bolted.

As my feet pounded down on the pavement, my arms and legs pumping, I was already regretting having parked my truck so far away. Why hadn't I just left it in the parking lot? It being parked on the main street wouldn't have drawn suspicion. Even Charlotte would have known I could just be shopping, if she'd spotted it. That was a mistake I hoped I wouldn't end up paying for with my life.

To my relief, no ringing gunshot came from behind me. No bullet penetrated my back. Apparently my gamble about her ditching the gun had been a good one.

I heard Charlotte's feet pounding after me, but it didn't

sound like she was running in the same direction I was. It seemed more like she was running to my right. I risked a glance over my shoulder to check that my ears weren't deceiving me, and saw that she was headed towards a parked car. She paused only a second to unlock the vehicle when she reached it. As soon as she clambered inside, the engine roared to life. She must have chosen to flee town.

That was what I thought, at first, so I slowed down to watch her. But then her eyes met mine through the windshield and she made a cutting motion across her throat.

My stomach turned over, as I realized escape wasn't her plan after all. With a burst of renewed energy, I sped up and ran on as fast as I could, dodging parked vehicles and tall lampposts that cast the parking lot in a yellow glow. Out beyond the pools of light, night had descended and it was now pitch black.

The glare of headlights suddenly engulfed me, lighting me up like a beacon against the shadows. The roar of an engine grew louder and I looked back to see that Charlotte's car was coming right at me.

Which way should I jump? Left or right? And how could I time it so that Charlotte was too late to turn around and follow me? I could duck between the dark shapes of the few vehicles parked nearby, but then she'd be blocking my only exit. How long could I manage to evade her? Not long, I suspected.

As I kept looking back, unable to tear my gaze from the car racing toward me, a dense white fog suddenly clouded my vision, seemingly coming from nowhere to fill the parking lot. It didn't drift in from the side, and it didn't slowly drop down from the sky above. Instead, it materialised out of thin air. One moment it wasn't there, the next moment it was.

I knew instinctively that this was Clayton's ghost somehow helping me from the other side. He was giving me cover and a chance to escape, and I didn't want to waste it. I veered left, running towards where I believed the entrance to the parking lot was, though it was hard to be sure through all this mist.

I had barely covered a few yards when I heard a loud screech of tires, followed by a deafening smashing sound directly behind me. I risked another glance over my shoulder. The thick fog in my wake had evaporated as quickly as it came, giving me a surprising view. Charlotte's car was wrapped around a lamppost, the windshield cracked, the engine dead, and the hood concertinaed in on itself. She must have crashed while blinded by the fog.

I could see Charlotte slumped over the steering wheel, the stillness of her body telling me she was either unconscious or worse. I wanted nothing more than to just keep running, but I realized leaving her here without help would make me almost as bad as her.

I approached the car cautiously. When I peered in the window, I could see Charlotte's shoulders rising and falling with her breaths. She was alive then and just out cold.

I got my cell phone out and placed a call to 911, requesting an ambulance. I called Tucker and then texted Billy, for good measure. While I stood waiting for help to arrive on the scene, I never took my eyes off Charlotte. I half-expected her to wake suddenly, scramble out of the wrecked car, and make a break for it. But that didn't happen.

19

———

Everything that happened after my confrontation with Charlotte, like waiting for help to show up and explaining everything to the police when they got there, all of it passed by in a blur. Something about nearly losing my life that night left me so dizzy that I didn't stop to think about the details until much later, after I made it home and found myself finally safe in my bed in my cozy attic room.

Nearly a full twenty-four hours later, I was still filled with anxious excitement, although this time it was a different kind. I stood at the entrance to the carnival, nervously hopping from foot to foot. I was early and had known I'd have to hang around and wait. But I'd had too much anxious energy to remain on the farm trying to make small talk with my grandparents.

I wasn't at the carnival to work tonight. No, I was here to meet Billy. Whether for a date or for an official breakup, I wasn't sure. I hoped for it to be a date, but suspected something less pleasant.

Last night, when I had waited with Charlotte for the

authorities to arrive, Billy had been among the first on the scene. He had looked at me strangely, his face wearing an expression I couldn't place. He'd started to say something but Tucker and a deputy had pulled up then, cutting him short. Billy had hurried to check on Charlotte and busied himself with helping her until the ambulance arrived. After the paramedics had taken the still-unconscious woman away, Billy had told me we needed to talk and asked me to meet him here tonight.

That was why I was of two minds as to what this meeting would be about. I knew the ghost thing had hit my boyfriend hard. Even if he could get past that, I didn't think he would be able to accept me getting drawn into dangerous investigations. And so, it was likely he had invited me here to end it all face-to-face. It was typical of Billy to do it courteously like that. On the other hand, would he really take me to a loud, public place like a carnival to break up? Wouldn't he want a conversation that awkward to happen in private?

I just didn't know, and it was the not knowing that was driving me slowly towards insanity. As much as I didn't want to lose Billy for good, if that was what was going to happen, I would rather learn the truth quickly and get on with my life.

I forced myself to think about something else. My mind automatically went back to last night. Billy had worked on Charlotte, stopping her bleeding until the ambulance had arrived. I had spoken to Tucker earlier in the day and he'd confirmed Charlotte would make a full recovery, and that she had confessed to everything and would stand trial for the murder of Clayton Caldwell. He sounded pretty certain she would be found guilty. Although I had little confidence in Tucker, I knew with Charlotte's confession and the evidence stacked against her, she had little chance of wriggling out of the charges.

That part at least had turned out well. Clayton had gotten the justice he so badly craved, and he would be able to rest in peace now. Or at least, rest in the closest state to peace a man so disagreeable could be in. I had seen no sign of him since the fog had cleared in the parking lot, so it seemed his ghost had already moved on.

Thinking about solving the murder led me to think about the other people I had briefly suspected of being Clayton's killer. Sam Hanson had now been cleared of any wrongdoing and no doubt the lawsuit against him would go away too. And then there was Mildred Benson, an old woman who loved her simple life, and was compassionate enough to invite a stranger into her home when they weren't feeling well. How could I ever have suspected her of being capable of murder? I guessed that Tucker was right on that score. Sometimes a button was just a button and not a clue. I suspected that whatever happened to the bookstore and the apartment above it now, Mildred Benson would be just fine. In the brief time I had known her, she had seemed to me like a survivor.

A hand landed on my shoulder, startling me and pulling me from my thoughts. I turned around to see Billy smiling sheepishly at me.

"Sorry. I didn't mean to startle you. I thought you would have heard me coming," he said.

I tried not to focus on the way his dark eyes and familiar smile set my heart to racing, Under the circumstances, it was best not to notice so much.

To hide my nerves, I said, "It's fine. I was just thinking about what will happen to old Mildred Benson now. She was Clayton's assistant in the store, and she lived above it. It would be a shame to see her kicked out of her home."

Billy and I started walking into the crowd at the carnival. I let him lead, following his path, still unsure of what this was.

He glanced at me and smiled. "Funny you should mention Mildred Benson. I spoke to Tucker earlier. He said he heard a rumor that Clayton Caldwell's will contained a real surprise when it was read today. It seems Clayton left Mildred the bookstore and the apartment with it."

"Really? That's perfect," I said.

I couldn't imagine what had inspired such generosity in an otherwise unpleasant man. Maybe Clayton wasn't all bad, after all. I could imagine how happy Mildred must have been when she heard the news.

I realized Billy had stopped walking and I stopped too. I looked up in surprise to see we were in line for the Ferris wheel. I looked at him questioningly.

"What? I thought the Ferris wheel was your favorite thing at the carnival," he said.

He wore a worried expression, like he was nervous about something.

"It is," I agreed. "But you said we needed to talk, and we do."

"Next please," the ride operator shouted and I found myself being ushered forward.

Not wanting to cause a scene, I got into a car beside Billy. The operator closed the safety bar and we were whisked up a notch.

"We do need to talk," Billy confirmed. "Well, actually I need to talk and I need you to just listen. Can you do that?"

I nodded, already mute. Was he really going to do this here and now? It would ruin the Ferris wheel forever for me, but I just wanted him to get it over with so I could finally know the truth. It would be worse to endure the whole ride not knowing what was coming after it.

"When you told me about the ghosts, I reacted badly, Emma. I want to apologise for that."

I shrugged. "It's fine. I kind of expected you to freak out. Most people would. I thought we would have at least talked about it, though."

Billy nodded, not looking at me. "I know. I'm sorry. That's what we should have done. And I'll be honest with you now. I still don't like the idea of you putting yourself in danger for any reason. But, here's the thing."

The car was swept up another notch and I felt my stomach roll as Billy went on. I wasn't sure if it was the motion of the Ferris wheel pulling me higher and higher, or the effect of Billy's words. Maybe it was a bit of both.

"I spent some time wondering if I could be with you despite all of that stuff. Once I had a chance to really think about it, I realized something. I don't want to be with you in spite of the ghosts and the danger you're always so quick to throw yourself into."

My heart started to break as we went up again.

"I want to be with you *because* of those things. It's a part of you, Emma, and I love all of you."

We lurched up again and Billy finally turned to look at me as my jaw dropped open in shock.

"So you're not breaking up with me?" I asked.

He smiled and touched my cheek.

"On the contrary. I'm saying I love you, Emma. You're the most amazing and surprising woman I have ever met."

I swallowed hard. Was everything really going to be okay?

"And you're willing to accept all of this?" I asked.

He nodded. "If you're willing to accept me back after the way I treated you," he said.

"Of course I am." I grinned.

We lurched again, two notches from the very top now.

"That's good, because I have something important to ask you," Billy said.

He pushed his hand into his coat pocket and pulled out a small red box.

"Emma, I love your quirks and your sense of justice and morality. And I love that you charge into danger when you think it's the right thing to do. I also love your laugh and the way you blush when you're flustered. I love the way you always know just the right thing to say. My life is better with you in it."

We moved up another spot.

"Will you marry me?" Billy asked.

I was too stunned to do anything but open and close my mouth silently. No words would come out. From the lead-up, maybe I should have expected this question was coming, but somehow I hadn't.

He opened the box, showing me the diamond ring inside. I didn't need to see the ring. I already knew my answer. It was just a question of getting my tongue to say the words.

"Yes," I screamed, finally finding my voice.

Tears of joy poured down my face as Billy took the ring from the box and slipped it onto my finger. I leaned forward and our lips met as we moved to the very top of the Ferris wheel.

We broke apart and grinned at each other. Billy slipped his arm around me and I shuffled closer to him, resting my head on his shoulder. As I looked down at the lights of the carnival, and further afield to the peaceful town beyond and the lights of Hillbilly Hollow, I knew one thing for sure. I had never been happier than I was in that moment.

I was no longer a city girl. I was a country girl through and through. I wondered what the future held for Billy and me, for Suzy and Brian, for my grandparents, and for the other residents of the Hollow. Whatever it was, I was ready for it. With Billy by my side, I was ready for anything.

The Ferris wheel started up again, catching me by surprise. My stomach lurched as we plummeted towards the ground, and I laughed with delight, hope and wonder. That was exactly how I felt about the next chapter of my life.

Continue following the ghostly mysteries and eccentric characters of Hillbilly Hollow in
"A Puzzling Plot in Hillbilly Hollow."

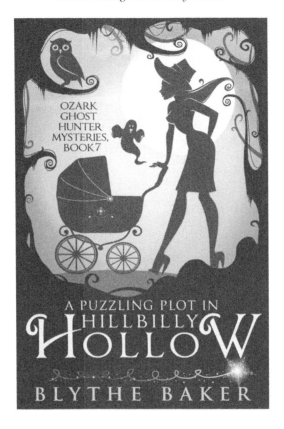

ABOUT THE AUTHOR

Blythe Baker is a thirty-something bottle redhead from the South Central part of the country. When she's not slinging words and creating new worlds and characters, she's acting as chauffeur to her children and head groomer to her household of beloved pets.

Blythe enjoys long walks with her dog on sweaty days, grubbing in her flower garden, cooking, and ruthlessly de-cluttering her overcrowded home. She also likes binge-watching mystery shows on TV and burying herself in books about murder.

To learn more about Blythe, visit her website and sign up for her newsletter at www.blythebaker.com